THE COLD PEOPLE

Don't miss any of the chilling adventures!

SPOOKSVILLE

THE
COLD
PEOPLE

Christopher Pike

Aladdin

NEW YORK LONDON TORONTO SYDNEY NEW DELHI

ALADDIN

An imprint of Simon & Schuster Children's Publishing Division
1230 Avenue of the Americas, New York, NY 10020
First Aladdin edition February 2015
Copyright © 1996 by Christopher Pike
Cover illustration © 2015 by Vivienne To
All rights reserved, including the right of reproduction
in whole or in part in any form.
ALADDIN is a trademark of Simon & Schuster, Inc.,
and related logo is a registered trademark of Simon & Schuster, Inc.
For information about special discounts for bulk purchases,
please contact Simon & Schuster Special Sales at 1-866-506-1949
or business@simonandschuster.com.
Cover designed by Jessica Handelman
Interior designed by Mike Rosamilia
The text of this book was set in Weiss Std.
Manufactured in the United States of America 0115 OFF
2 4 6 8 10 9 7 5 3 1
This title has been cataloged with the Library of Congress.
ISBN 978-1-4814-1061-8 (pbk)
ISBN 978-1-4814-1067-0 (hc)
ISBN 978-1-4814-1068-7 (eBook)

1

It was another Spooksville mystery.

The town was freezing, and it was summer still. The cold weather was as strange as the boiling temperatures of a couple weeks earlier, when Adam Freeman and his friends had run into aliens. None of them could understand what had brought on the chilly snap. That Monday morning—when they first got up—every window in town was coated with a fine layer of white frost. Little did they know that by the time the sun went down, there would be frost *inside* many of the people who lived in Spooksville.

Adam, Sally Wilcox, Cindy Makey, and Watch started off the day by having their usual milk and doughnuts at the local bakery. Actually, because of the cold, they each had a cup of coffee as well, just to warm their bones. Watch had a thermometer in one of the four watches he regularly wore, and he studied it as they munched their food. He said he doubted the temperature would get above freezing all day.

"It's still in the low twenties," he added. "If we're going to be outside today, we'd better keep moving."

They took Watch's suggestion to heart and decided to spend the day hiking in the woods in the hills around Spooksville. They pedaled their bikes until the road ran out and then hid them in some trees. Adam had been up in the hills before, of course, when he visited the Haunted Cave and the reservoir. But he had never been into the woods. He was amazed at the size and variety of the trees.

"This forest is like something out of *Hansel and Gretel*," he said as they hiked along a narrow path covered with pine needles. He wore a heavy jacket, which he unzipped as he walked. The exercise was taking away some of the chill.

Sally snorted. "Hansel and Gretel were lightweights. They had only one witch to kill, and they got famous. We get worse than that every week and no one writes about us."

"We need a press agent," Watch agreed. "Our life stories need to be on TV."

"Personally I like being unknown," Cindy said. "I don't need all the money and fame."

"Wait till you're a few years older," Sally said. "Money and fame will be what you crave most."

"I think all that stuff is superficial," Cindy said.

Sally snickered. "Spoken like a true liberal. In this world you've got to cash in on whatever, whenever you can. For that reason I've started to keep a journal of my experiences. If I don't die in the next ten years, I figure I'll be able to auction the movie rights to my life."

"Am I in your journal?" Adam asked.

Sally hesitated. "You're mentioned in a small footnote."

It was Cindy's turn to snicker. "I bet the whole journal is about Adam."

"That's not true," Sally said quickly.

"Ha," Cindy said. "Prove it. Let us read it."

"You can read it," Sally said. "In exchange for a million bucks."

As usual, Sally had the last word. They continued up the path without further conversation. The path narrowed as the trees grew thicker and pushed in from the sides. The way the heavy branches hung over them, it could have been close to dark—the shade was that deep. Yet Adam could still make out his breath as he exhaled. Once again he wondered about the strange weather, and what could be causing it. He knew there must be a reason.

They were finished exploring and about to turn back when they spotted the Cold People. Adam saw them first, but thought he was just seeing huge blocks of ice jammed between trees. That in itself would have been strange. Even though there was frost, there was no actual snow or ice.

"Hey," Adam said, pointing to a spot fifty feet off the path. "What's that?"

They all peered in the shadows.

"Looks like a glacier," Sally said.

"The ice age would have to arrive for us to have a glacier here," Cindy said.

"This town is not known for standard weather patterns," Sally said. "Two winters ago we had an iceberg float into our harbor. It hung offshore for a couple of months. We had incredible snowball fights, until a polar bear came out of a hidden ice cave and ate Buddy Silverstone."

Cindy snorted. "I don't believe it."

"There actually was an iceberg," Watch said. "But it was an Eskimo who came out of the cave. And he just invited Buddy to dinner."

"Yeah, but he didn't tell Buddy that he was the main course," Sally lied.

"Would you guys stop arguing and tell me what we're looking at," Adam said.

Cindy squinted. "Looks like big blocks of ice."

"We know that," Sally said impatiently. "But what is the nature of these blocks of ice? Are they composed of frozen water? Are they from this planet? You have to ask yourself these questions."

"Why don't we walk over and have a closer look," Watch suggested.

It was a reasonable idea, although it was harder to get to the ice blocks than Adam would have imagined. The trees were so dense that he felt as if they were threatening to squeeze him to a pulp. No pun intended, he thought. But he realized he must be flashing back on his first day in Spooksville, when a tree had, in fact, tried to eat him alive. He had thought at the time that that was a strange day. Looking back, it had been pretty normal for Spooksville.

There were not the two or three blocks of ice they had seen from the path, but literally dozens. Some were lying down, others stood jammed between tree trunks. They were almost all identical in size, seven feet long by two feet deep and wide. Adam and his friends knelt by the first one they came to—which was lying flat. Watch tried brushing off the outer covering of frost. But still they could not see to the center of it.

Yet they could make out something in there.

Something large and dark.

"These are shaped like frozen coffins," Sally said softly.

"Where did they come from?" Cindy whispered, fear in her voice. Up close, the ice blocks were sort of scary. Watch continued to brush at the outer frost, probably hoping to clear the ice.

"I don't think the ice-cream man put them here," Sally said.

"This block is really cold," Watch said, pausing to breathe on his unprotected hand. "And I don't mean it's ice-cold."

"What do you mean?" Cindy asked.

"Let me show you," Watch said. He took off the watch that had the thermometer and laid it on top of the block. He left it there for perhaps ten seconds before he snapped it back up. He studied the reading. "Ten degrees Fahrenheit," he muttered.

"That's twenty-two degrees below freezing," Sally whispered, amazed.

"That's a lot colder than the air temperature ever gets around here," Adam said.

Watch nodded. "Unless these blocks were just dropped here a few minutes ago—which I doubt—

something inside them is generating this incredible cold." He tapped at the block with the knuckles of his right hand, then leaned over and sniffed it. "I don't even think this is frozen water."

"What is it, then?" Cindy asked.

Watch frowned. "It has a faint ammonia smell. But it's not ammonia." He glanced at Adam. "I'd like to thaw one of these out."

"Do you think that's a good idea?" Adam asked.

"No," Sally and Cindy said quickly together. They glanced at each other in surprise. They seldom agreed on anything. Sally continued, "There may be something inside we don't want thawed out."

"Like what?" Adam asked.

Sally shook her head. "You know this town. We could have anything from a bloodthirsty vampire to a blob from Planet Zeon inside here. I have a personal rule against fooling with any strange artifact that might end up eating me."

"That rule must make your journal pretty boring," Cindy remarked.

"There's a problem here that we're forgetting," Adam said. "It's freezing today, and it's still summer. These blocks are colder than freezing. So is it possible there's a connection between the two?"

Watch nodded. "Good point. But I know for a fact that these blocks alone are not cooling off the entire town."

"I'm not saying that," Adam replied. "What I mean is these blocks may have come here today because it's cold."

"You mean whoever put them here might be making it cold?" Cindy asked.

"Exactly," Adam said.

"I think we have to take a chance," Watch said. "We have to thaw one out. Maybe there's nothing inside any of these blocks."

"I have my Bic lighter," Sally said reluctantly. "We could gather some dry sticks and build a fire beside it."

"But the fire might hurt whatever is inside the block," Cindy said.

"Personally, I'm not worried about that," Sally said.

"If we're careful with the flames," Watch said, "I'm sure we can avoid damaging the contents of the block."

Adam nodded. "I do think we have to have a look at the inside. I know I won't be able to sleep wondering what's in it. As long as we all understand that we probably won't be able to freeze the block again."

Sally nodded. "This is like opening Pandora's box. There might be no way to close the box."

2

THEY DIDN'T HAVE TO GO FAR TO GATHER
sticks and twigs to build a fire. Even though it was cold,
the ground was dry. Soon they had a respectable pile of
wood beside the ice block. Sally took out her lighter.

"Why do you carry a lighter?" Cindy asked. "Are you
thinking of taking up smoking?"

Sally made a face. "You will recall how many times
we wished we had a lighter in the last four weeks.
Spooksville is unpredictable. If I wasn't such a pacifist,
I'd carry a gun in my other pocket."

Cindy smiled. "You're as much of a pacifist as a hungry mountain lion is."

"What does *pacifist* mean?" Adam asked Watch.

"Sally when she's totally unconscious," Watch replied. "Light the pile, Sally, and move back. Adam, Cindy—you get back too. I'll take care of the fire."

Sally flicked her Bic. In the deep shadows from the surrounding trees, the orange flame glowed bright. Sally moved it toward the pile of sticks and twigs.

"Are you worried something might jump out and grab us?" Sally asked.

"There's no reason to risk all of us," Watch said.

The flame caught immediately. In seconds they had a crackling campfire. The dark smoke gathered beneath the frost-covered branches. As the white flakes thawed, drops of water fell around them. But the block of ice thawed much more slowly. Taking Watch's advice, Adam had moved back a few feet. But he could see that the block was hardly reacting to the fire. He pointed it out to the others.

"Just what I suspected," Watch said. "This block can't be frozen water. It must be some other substance, with a much lower freezing point. Hand me a couple of those logs, Cindy. We need a bigger fire if we're going to get anywhere with this thing today."

So Watch threw a couple of *real* logs on the fire. This wood took a few minutes to catch, but soon they had a roaring fire going. The smoke continued to gather beneath the branches, creating a black cloud that caused them all to start coughing. But now, finally, the block started to melt.

The liquid, as it dripped off, was a dull blue.

It puddled around Watch. Steam rose from it. Blue steam. It mingled with the black smoke, creating a ghostly color.

The block started to become clearer.

There was definitely something inside.

Humanoid shaped. It could be a man.

A very cold man.

"Watch," Adam said softly. "I think maybe you should sit back with us."

"Yeah," Sally whispered. "I don't like what I'm seeing."

Watch shook his head. "I have to control the fire. I can't burn him."

"Is it a *him?*" Cindy gasped.

"I think so," Watch said. "And if it is a person, he's got to be dead. He can't hurt us."

"I wouldn't necessarily make that statement about dead people in Spooksville," Sally said.

The ice—or whatever it was—continued to thaw. A hand became visible inside the block, then an arm. The latter plopped out as the heat of the flames dug deeper into the block. The exposed flesh glistened in the light from the fire. Soon they were staring at a man. He was not naked but wore what looked like a blue jump suit. Yet his skin was very pale. Of course, he was a corpse—he was supposed to be pale.

"Is he alive?" Sally asked.

"He was frozen," Cindy said. "He can't be alive." She paused. "Is he alive?"

Watch carefully poked his skin. "I don't think so. He's not moving or breathing and he's too cold."

"I don't think you should touch him," Adam said. "He might not like it."

"Dead people don't like or dislike anything," Cindy said.

"I know a few dead people who have very specific tastes," Sally said. "But I agree with Adam. Don't touch him. You might catch some disease."

Watch ignored them. He picked up the hand and studied the palm. "Incredible," he whispered. "There are no lines on this hand. No prints on the fingers."

"But aren't fingerprints created in the womb?" Adam said.

"Yes," Watch said. "I don't think this creature was ever in one."

"What are you saying?" Cindy demanded.

"He's saying this creature was never born," Sally said,

her tone anxious. "And if that's the case, it might never have died. Watch, get away from it *now*. You're making me nervous."

It was a pity Watch didn't take Sally's advice. If he had, maybe he would have gotten away. Maybe they all would have. But there were many maybe-mysteries in Spooksville that were never solved. Watch didn't listen and he didn't get away.

Watch was poking at the palm when the hand came alive.

The fingers moved. They bent into a claw shape.

Watch dropped the hand and sat back.

But the cold man's arm was long.

It reached out and grabbed Watch by the foot.

"It's got me!" Watch cried as he tried to shake loose. "Help!"

They jumped to his side, crowding around the fire. Adam went down on his knees beside Watch's foot and pried at the fingers with all his strength. But they were like marble and didn't budge. The hand began to pull Watch toward the block of ice. Sally grabbed a stick and began to pound on it. Cindy kicked at it. Still, the cold arm continued to drag Watch in toward the block.

"Grab a stick out of the fire!" Watch shouted. "Press it to its skin!"

Unfortunately they all turned to follow Watch's advice at once. Which was a shame because at that exact moment, when their backs were to the block of ice, it exploded. The shards of ice fell over them like debris from a blast. For a moment they didn't even know what was happening.

But then they saw that the cold man had broken free. It was standing straight up. Holding on to Watch.

The cold man opened its eyes and stared at them.

The eyes were blue, completely blue. There were no pupils, no eyelashes. They shone with a strange light that sent shivers down their backs. The creature had its arm around Watch's neck. Clearly it had no intention of letting him go.

"Use the fire," Watch rasped, shivering uncontrollably. "Try to force him to release me."

"Maybe we could ask it to let you go," Cindy cried. "Hey, you big Popsicle, let our friend go!"

In response the creature only stared at Cindy, and the strange blue light from its eyes seemed to envelope her. Cindy backed up and screamed.

"It's freezing me!" she said.

Adam had seen enough. He had a burning stick in his hand. He rushed toward the creature, waving it in the air. The cold creature turned away from Cindy and retreated. But it continued to hold on to Watch, using him as a shield.

"Let him go or you burn!" Adam shouted. "Sally! Go around his back."

"Gotcha," Sally said, a burning stick in her hand as well. She split from Adam's side and tried to get behind the creature. But the trees were too thick, so she only made it to his right side. The cold man's head darted from side to side. Clearly it didn't like the fire, yet it was willing to risk it to hold on to Watch. Every time Adam tried to make a stab at the thing with his torch, it blocked his way using Watch as a shield.

"What should I do?" Adam called to Watch.

"It's so cold," Watch moaned, his lips actually turning white, as if he were freezing to death. "Try threatening one of its partners."

"I'm on that," Cindy said, grabbing a particularly big burning branch and taking it over to another block of ice. She held it close to the ice and called back to the cold man. "Let him go or I fry this one!"

Once more the cold man concentrated its weird glowing eyes on Cindy. The blue light seemed to leap toward her. Before Cindy could even raise her torch to ward off the freezing beam, her arm grew numb. She tried to speak but only choked sounds came out. Adam thought she might freeze or suffocate in the next minute. Not having a chance to think of another plan, he threw his torch in the air, at the creature's head. The torch landed behind it, and the cold man turned and was forced to withdraw its icy gaze. But this time it didn't give them a chance to regroup.

Tightening its grip on Watch, it yanked him into the trees. It was very quick and out of sight before any of them could react.

In the shadows of the forest, they heard Watch scream.

Then there was nothing but silence. Horrible silence. The cold man had taken their friend.

3

THEY PUT OUT THE FIRE. THE FLAMES APPEARED to be their only defense, but they were afraid the heat might wake another of the creatures. Yet they kept their torches, and they went after Watch.

But it was hopeless from the start. The trees were so crowded that it took them half an hour to go a hundred yards. Plus the creature could move many times faster than they could. They trudged after their friend with heavy hearts, knowing they weren't going to find him, not without help. As they paused to catch their breath beside a gurgling stream, Adam stared at the dying torches and shook his head.

"We have to go back to the path," he said reluctantly.

"We can't face the cold man without fire, and these sticks will burn out in a few minutes."

"But we can't leave Watch," Cindy cried. "Remember when we were trapped in the cave? He did everything he could to rescue us. We have to do the same for him."

"I agree with Adam," Sally said sadly. "We can't help him this way. We need reinforcements, better weapons. We have to get back to town and warn everybody about what could happen."

"No one will believe us," Cindy said. "If you told me a creature's gaze could freeze me, I wouldn't believe it."

"But you don't believe anything I say," Sally replied.

"We'll have to deal with that problem when we come to it," Adam said.

"But what are we going to tell people?" Cindy persisted. "We don't even know what these creatures are. We have no idea where they come from."

Sally was curious. "What was it like when the creature stared at you?"

Cindy lowered her head and shivered. "It was as if the blood in my veins were turning to ice—literally. And there was something else—it was like the cold man hated me for being warm. I felt its hate, its envy." A tear slipped over her cheek. "I hope Watch is all right." She raised her head and stared at Adam. "You think he's still alive, don't you?"

Adam wanted to say something encouraging but knew Cindy would see through his lie. He thought of how strong the cold man was, how quickly it moved. How powerful its strange eyes were. Adam didn't have much hope for his friend.

"I just don't know," Adam said quietly.

Their bikes were still where they'd left them. The road back to town was mostly downhill, and they never pedaled so fast in all their lives. The cold wind stung their faces, their cheeks burning and freezing at the same time. Adam wanted to ride straight to the police station but Sally wanted to find Bum first.

"Bum knows a thousand times more than the police do," she said.

"I thought you didn't trust Bum," Adam said.

"I trust no one," Sally said. "But Bum likes Watch. He'll do anything to rescue him."

They found Bum, who had once been the mayor of Spooksville, down at the beach feeding the pigeons. He seemed happy to see them, but when they told him what had happened, he sat down with a weary thud. His glum expression worried them. They could have come to tell him about the breakout of the next world war and he might have laughed it off. He was that easygoing.

But there was something in their story that touched him deeply.

"It's the Cryo Creatures," Bum muttered.

"What are they?" Adam demanded.

"Cryo means cold," Sally offered.

"We know that," Cindy said impatiently. "But what are these creatures?"

Bum sighed. "To put it bluntly, they're bad news. I haven't heard of them in a long time. In fact, they have never appeared during my lifetime before." He paused and shook his head. "You say they got Watch?"

"Yeah, one of them does," Adam said. "What will it do to him?"

"Make him cold," Bum said softly.

"That's all?" Cindy asked hopefully. "It won't kill him?"

Bum put his hand to his head. "You misunderstand me. It would be better if it did kill him. When I say it will make him cold, I mean it will make him like itself."

Sally's face fell. "You mean it will turn Watch into a monster?"

Bum spoke darkly. "By now it has already changed him. There is no Watch anymore. If you see him, he will try to change you."

Adam felt his heart breaking. "But can Watch be changed back into a human?"

Bum rubbed his head. He appeared to be thinking hard about what to do.

"I don't know," he said. "I don't think so. These Cryo Creatures—they're ancient, and their power is very great. We may all be doomed." He nodded to the ground beside the ocean wall where he sat. "Make yourselves comfortable. I have a story to tell you. It isn't a pleasant story, but you have to hear it if you're to know what you're dealing with."

Adam sat, even though he desperately wanted to rush off and save Watch. "Can you give us the short version? We have to try to help Watch, no matter what you tell us."

"You can help him most by listening for a few minutes," Bum said. "But what I have to say—you don't have to believe any of it if you don't want to. I won't care. You can just see the story as a myth. But I can tell you that I believe it."

Bum paused to clear his throat. As he told his story, he stared out at the ocean.

"A long time ago the world was not as it is now. You have probably heard of the lost continent of Atlantis, which was located in the Atlantic Ocean. Atlantis really did exist. During the same time period there was another land that has since vanished. This one was in the Pacific Ocean and was called Lemuria, or Mu for short. It was twice the size of Atlantis. You may be surprised to know that parts of the West Coast were once parts of Mu. Spooksville, for example, used to be an eastern city of Mu. I have often thought that one of the reasons Spooksville is such an unusual place is because it really belongs to another time and place. But that's a story for another time.

"Atlantis and Mu existed for tens of thousands of years, but the two peoples were not always on the best of terms. Actually, they spent a lot of time fighting. But they had so much history together, they were also friendly for long centuries at a time. Still, they could never remain friendly. The main reason was that they were never left alone. You see, in those days the technology was far more advanced than it is today. They had machines that could beam you from one side of the planet to the other. Ships that could travel to other galaxies.

"I know in school your history teachers never talk about these things. Few people in the world realize how old civilization really is. How old mankind is. You see, we did not originate on Earth, but came from a star cluster called the Pleiades, or the Seven Sisters as it is commonly called. You can see it in the winter sky if you look up on a dark night. The cluster is hundreds of light-years from Earth. Our most ancient ancestors came from worlds that circled those blue stars in the Pleiades. But the people of the Pleiades originally came from somewhere else. From a world that was long ago destroyed. No one can really say where it all started.

"People from the Pleiades and other worlds often visited Earth. Their spaceships landed in Atlantis and in Mu. The trouble was that the same star people didn't visit Mu and Atlantis. There are many Pleiades worlds, dozens. They didn't all get along either. I don't know how they're doing these days. The witch—Ann Templeton—might know. Some say Madeline Templeton, Ann's great-great-great-great-great grandmother, was from one of those worlds. But that, too, is another story.

"So we had these two large lands, Mu and Atlantis, and they were being told what to do by different races. And these different star races didn't like each other. Toward the end of Atlantis and Mu, the star people were at war, and they wanted the people of Earth to join their war. These different races from Pleiades saw the Earth as just another battlefield. It was a mess. The scientists from one planet were telling the people of Atlantis how to make a bomb to blow up Mu, while other star scientists were telling the people of Mu how to blow up Atlantis."

Adam interrupted. "Why didn't the people of Earth just tell these guys to get in their spaceships and fly away and leave them alone?"

Bum nodded. "That's a good question. The reason the Earth people didn't kick them out is that the star people knew more than they did. True, the Earth had originally been settled by the star people, but that had been millions of years before all this went on. By the time the star people returned and brought their troubles, people on Earth were way behind them. The star people had machines and devices that would have taken Earth people thousands of years to invent. I guess you could say the star people bribed the Earth people. 'If you do this for us,' they would say to our leaders, 'we will give you this secret.'"

"But what does all this have to do with the Cryo Creatures?" Sally asked.

"I'm just getting to that part. I had to explain these other things first." Again Bum paused to clear his throat. Actually, he sounded hoarse. Adam wondered if he had a cold. Adam imagined that living outside all the time was not easy.

"I have to make clear that not all the star people were evil," Bum went on. "You know in any war there are good guys and bad guys. But I don't think in this war all the good guys were on one side. I think it was mixed. Many of the star people who helped Atlantis really thought they were doing the right thing. I'm sure many of the star people who helped Mu thought they were doing the right thing too. But I do know the star scientists on the Mu side made the Mu leaders a really evil offer. An offer so tempting that the Mu leaders could not resist."

"If it was an evil offer," Cindy said, "why was it so tempting?"

"Evil is always more tempting than good," Sally said. "That's life. All the fun things get you into trouble."

Bum paused and smiled, although he remained serious. "Sally might be right, I'm not sure. But I do know that one secret group from the Pleiades told the leaders of Mu that if they would completely wipe out Atlantis, they would be given a chance to live for tens of thousands of years."

Adam was impressed. "Did the star people live that long?"

Bum scratched his head. "They lived a very long time, much longer than Earth people. The leaders of Mu could see that. Each time the star people visited— every few years—they would hardly have aged at all, while the leaders would be getting old and wrinkled. These evil star people convinced the Mu leaders that they didn't have to die, which was a lie. Even the star people died, eventually. It was just another bribe, a false bribe. Yet there was truth in it as well. Let me explain.

"If you cool something down, it lasts longer. If you

freeze it, and keep it frozen, it lasts practically forever. You can do this with hamburger. Put it in the freezer in your refrigerator and you can eat it a year later. The meat won't spoil. But the second you take the meat out of the freezer, it thaws out and grows old. Leave it out for a few days and it will rot. Do you get my point?"

"Yes," Adam said. "But you can't freeze people to make them live forever. If you freeze people they can't move. They die."

"That's true with the technology we have now," Bum said. "But don't forget these visitors from the stars knew things we can't even imagine. They told the leaders of Mu that—in exchange for wiping out Atlantis—they would show them how to transform the cells of their bodies so that they lived on a frozen substance called Cryo instead of on warm blood. Don't ask me what this Cryo was made of—I don't know. But somehow it allowed a person to be colder than ice and yet walk around and act like a living person."

"Did any of the star people have Cryo in their veins?" Sally asked.

"That's another good question," Bum said. "The answer, as far as I know, was no. None of the star scientists visiting the Earth was a Cryo Creature. That should have warned the leaders of Mu that something was fishy.

But I think these leaders were all selfish people, cowards, afraid of death. They took the bribe. They thought they would wipe out Atlantis and in exchange they would be made immortal.

"It's not easy to destroy an entire continent. Even with nuclear bombs, you can't make a whole land mass vanish. What the leaders of Mu decided was to get a little help from the asteroid belt. You know, it's out in space between Mars and Jupiter—a bunch of huge rocks floating around the sun. These guys—they may have been evil but they were pretty clever. They hooked rockets and space drives onto a particular asteroid and began to steer it toward the Earth. They adjusted the speed and direction precisely. Just as Atlantis was coming around—as the Earth rotated—the asteroid was right there. Like a big rock flying right toward them.

"Of course the Atlantean people saw it coming. It darkened their entire sky. In the last hours they knew they were about to be wiped out and they guessed the leaders of Mu were behind it all. But what they didn't know was that those leaders weren't human anymore.

"But I have to back up for a moment. Once the Mu leaders had directed the asteroid toward Atlantis, they had fulfilled their part of the bargain. Never mind that the asteroid took a few weeks to reach the Earth. Even before it became visible in the sky, the evil star people drained the blood of each of the leaders of Mu and replaced it with Cryo. Then the star people quickly left. Maybe they left laughing."

"Why?" Adam interrupted, fascinated by the tale, even though he wasn't sure if he believed it. Bum was right—he had never read about any of these things in any history book. Then again, he hadn't gone to school in Spooksville yet. Maybe they had a whole class devoted to prehistory. Bum replied to his question seriously.

"Because the Cryo stopped the aging process in the leaders, but it did other things to them as well, some of which were not very pleasant. The leaders became super strong and super fast. They also gained strange visual powers. Not only could they see far away, they could freeze people by glancing at them. In fact, they could make others like themselves, if they wished.

"But the problem was they were not really alive. They didn't *feel* alive. They just felt cold all the time, and they hated the cold. They were like the walking dead. They envied normal people. True, they would live for a very long time, but they couldn't enjoy anything. They understood this right away, even before the asteroid reached the Earth. They realized they had been tricked by the evil star people.

"But back to the asteroid. Like I said, it was headed straight toward Atlantis and the people there knew who had aimed it at them. But despite all their technology, they couldn't stop it. An asteroid can be pretty big. This one was over twenty miles in diameter and it was traveling at hundreds of miles a minute. Sure, the people of Atlantis shot nuclear missiles at it, but it just kept coming, straight on course. They were in a real bind.

"They didn't want to lie down and die, at least not without getting revenge. Just as the asteroid began to near the atmosphere, they fired off every weapon they had at Mu. From coast to coast, Mu burned. When the asteroid did strike, Atlantis was crushed beneath the Atlantic Ocean. Worse, it was forced beneath the Earth's crust. That's why there is almost no sign of it these days. The geological plates of the Earth shifted under the blow of the asteroid. Mu, which was already burning, also slid under the Pacific Ocean. Both great lands were destroyed together. Both great civilizations were wiped out, and people don't even remember them today." Bum paused. "I think it's a sad story."

"But what about the Cryo Creatures?" Sally insisted. "They're our problem right now."

"Yeah," Adam said, although he had enjoyed the story. "Didn't they all die when Mu was destroyed?"

"No," Bum said. "Some of them escaped. From what I understand, several figured out ahead of time that Atlantis would attack before the asteroid hit. They left Mu and traveled to the North Pole, where they dug themselves into valleys of ice. They survived the fire from the bombs and the impact of the asteroid." Bum stopped. "But now they've come back."

"Why?" Adam asked. "Why here? Why today?"

Bum was thoughtful. "They may have come here because Spooksville is one of the few surviving pieces of Mu. But why they have come today, I don't know. From what you described, someone must have brought them here—since they were frozen solid. But who that someone was—your guess is as good as mine."

"All this is very interesting," Sally said. "But how do we stop them, other than blowing up all of Spooksville?"

Bum spoke seriously. "That might be the only way to stop them. This city is not the only place in danger. From what I know of their history, the Cold People could sweep over the entire world. It may have been a good thing Mu was destroyed when it was. Before the asteroid hit, the Cold People who remained in Mu were already altering their own people. They're like vampires, changing people to be like them."

"Look," Adam said, getting impatient. "We can't blow

up Spooksville. You have to give us a second option."

"You mentioned how the creature fled from the fire," Bum said. "That's a key right there. We have an army surplus store just outside of town that sells all kinds of exotic war equipment. They have a few flamethrowers. You might want to buy them."

"They're not going to sell flamethrowers to kids," Cindy protested.

"They might," Sally said. "I know the owner of the store, Mr. Patton. He stole his name from a famous World War Two general. He believes every man and woman should walk around armed at all times. He'll sell you a tank if you have the money."

Bum nodded. "He might even give you the equipment on credit, if he's convinced the city's really in danger."

"Aren't you going to come with us?" Sally asked. "We need your help if we're to fight these things."

Bum scratched his unshaven chin and thought a minute. "I would rather leave town and try to forget that any of this is happening."

"Coward," Cindy muttered under her breath.

Bum half-smiled. "I said I would rather leave. I didn't say that I would. Sure, I'll help you fight them. God knows if we don't stop them here, we'll never stop them." Bum stood. "Come on, let's get to the surplus store."

They all stood. But Cindy appeared to have reservations about their plan.

"Why don't we go to the police?" Cindy asked. "That's what they're here for—to help in times of emergency."

Sally snorted. "That may be true in other cities. But in Spooksville the police are afraid to answer a call to get a cat out of a tree. Too many of their buddies go out on calls and never return."

Cindy was doubtful. "I think we have to at least warn them. Adam, would you come with me? We can catch up with Sally and Bum in an hour or so."

"An hour is a long time when you're dealing with creatures that can multiply," Sally warned. "But of course Adam will go with his dear Cindy just because she asked. He does whatever she asks because he loves her, and she acts like she loves him. It doesn't matter that the safety of the entire world is at stake. Isn't that true, Adam?"

"Well," Adam said, caught off guard. "I think we should let the police know."

Sally and Bum exchanged knowing glances.

"We'll pick out the flamethrowers," Bum said.

"We'll have them gift wrapped before these guys show up," Sally agreed.

4

THE CHIEF OF POLICE OF SPRINGVILLE—THE
proper name of Spooksville—was alone in the station when they arrived. There wasn't even a secretary
around, never mind other officers. There was just the
chief sitting behind his big oak desk, reading a comic
book and eating a box of chocolates. From his wide
belly, it appeared he often ate lots of them.

They knocked before entering but nevertheless
startled him. He glanced up and nervously set aside
his comic book. He smoothed his blue tie, which was
stained with chocolate, and blinked behind his gold-
rimmed glasses. He was probably only fifty years old,
but his hair was snow-white.

"Yes," he said. "Can I help you?"

"Yes," Adam said. "The two of us and two other friends were hiking in the hills behind Spooks—Springville this morning when we came across these huge blocks of ice. We thawed one out and this creature—like a cold man—jumped out and grabbed our friend, Watch. He dragged Watch into the woods, and we haven't seen Watch since." Adam paused. "We need your help to rescue him."

The chief just stared at him for a minute. Then he offered each of them his box of chocolates. "Would you like one?" he asked.

"No thanks, we're not hungry," Cindy said. "We're too worried about our friend. Can you help us?"

The chief helped himself to another chocolate. He ate it slowly—chewing seemed to take all his concentration.

"I don't know," he said. "What do you want me to help you with?"

Adam felt exasperated. "We just told you. One of the Cold People kidnapped our friend. We want you to help us get him back."

The chief took off his glasses and cleaned them with a handkerchief. "I'm alone here today. Do you really expect me to leave the station unattended?"

Cindy gestured to the empty building. "Where are all the other police?"

The chief seemed puzzled by the question. "Well, I don't very well know where they are. I can't keep track of everything. But years ago, when I started here, we had many fine officers. But their numbers have dwindled over time. Actually, I haven't seen another officer in the last few months." He paused to think. "It may have been in the last year."

"But what do you do if there's an emergency?" Cindy asked.

"What am I supposed to do? I have problems of my own. I have to run this whole station all by myself. If I leave, what will become of it?"

"But you can't help anyone if you're sitting in here," Cindy said, annoyed. "You just grow fat eating chocolates all day."

The chief was insulted. "Watch your tongue, young lady. I offered you a chocolate fair and square and you turned it down. Why shouldn't I eat it? If I don't, it will go to waste. I don't just throw away chocolates and pretend it's not wrong."

"We're not talking about chocolates," Adam said, trying once more, although he was beginning to see that it was hopeless. "We're talking about our friend. His life may be in danger. Can't you do anything to help him?"

The chief leaned over and peered at them. "Does he have life insurance?"

"What?" Adam said. "I don't know. What does that have to do with anything?"

The chief smiled in a condescending manner. "Young man, if he has insurance, and he is killed, his family will stand to gain financially. And in these troubled times, extra income is nothing to be taken lightly. In other words, you view this as an emergency, but this might be a blessing in disguise. Certainly I would be doing your friend's family a disservice if I prevented them from receiving a large amount of money. So you see my hands are tied by my responsibilities to this station and my moral duty to this young man's family."

"How can you talk about moral duty?" Cindy asked. "When you're too much of a coward to lift a finger to save him?"

The chief lost his smile. "You call me a coward? You have a lot of nerve. Have I ever come to you for help to find one of *my* friends? Of course not. I attend to my own problems. You should do likewise, and quit bothering good people who just want to be left alone."

"But you're a police officer," Cindy said bitterly. "It's your job to help people."

That took the chief back a step. He had to think for

a moment before answering. Before he did, however, he helped himself to another chocolate.

"There was nothing in my contract with the city that specified that I was to have to deal with mysterious Cold People," he said. "If there was, I would have had my lawyer strike it from my list of responsibilities. I don't even like the cold. That's another reason why I don't want to go outside today. I might catch cold, and then where would this fine city be?"

"Probably no worse off," Adam muttered. He turned toward the exit. "Come on, Cindy. Sally was right. We're wasting our time here."

But Cindy was too frustrated to walk away. Stepping up to the chief's desk, she suddenly reached out and grabbed his box of chocolates. Before he could stop her, she dropped it upside-down on the dusty floor, ruining the candies. The chief stared at her in shock, but Cindy smiled sweetly.

"We have an emergency situation," she said. "Now you do too. How does it feel?"

Adam grabbed her arm and dragged her toward the door before the chief could react. Adam was worried the man would throw her in jail.

"I think you've been hanging out with Sally too long," Adam told her.

5

THE OWNER OF THE SURPLUS STORE, MR. Patton, was dressed in full combat uniform. As Adam and Cindy entered his store, he was sitting on the floor, slipping bullets into an assault rifle clip. He was approximately thirty-five, blond, with the muscles of a Marine. It looked like Bum and Sally had been talking to him about the Cold People. He wore a twisted grin. The battle he had been preparing for all his life had finally arrived.

"'Welcome," he said. "Grab yourself a weapon and prepare to hit the front lines."

"Our friends told you what's happening?" Adam asked.

"Sure did." Mr. Patton finished loading the machine

gun and jumped up and grabbed a grenade launcher off the shelf. "The day of reckoning has finally arrived, like I always knew it would."

"Excuse me," Adam said. "But I don't know if these creatures can be stopped by bullets."

Mr. Patton flashed them a wild, red-eyed look. "That machine gun there is an M16. It can fire a sixteen-bullet clip in less than five seconds. I get a lock on one of those creatures with that baby, I guarantee you the creature is going down."

Adam shrugged. "Well, I don't know much about guns."

"I do," Cindy said. "My mother says they are disgusting and immoral."

Mr. Patton laughed. "People always say those kind of things until real trouble shows up. You try stopping a bear with a white flag and it will just have you for lunch. It's a jungle out there, I tell you." He gestured toward the rear of the store. "Your friends are in the back. I'm sure they agree with me. I think they're juicing up a couple of flamethrowers."

"I'm sure Sally would agree with you," Adam said, stepping toward the back of the store.

"But she's crazy," Cindy added.

They did find Sally and Bum in the back. Adam was surprised to see the store had its own supply of gasoline.

Sally and Bum were fueling a couple of flamethrowers, and filling a couple of spare tanks of fuel. The hand-held weapons looked like rocket launchers, except they spouted fire rather than explosives. Sally already had one going, but with the power down low. The orange flame danced like a hyperactive lighter. Sally's eyes gleamed as she stared at the burning tip.

"Let them try to grab one of us now," she said.

"Don't forget how fast they move," Adam warned.

"*They?*" Cindy said. "There's only one that's thawed out."

"We have to figure they're all up and running around by now," Bum said.

"Oh, no," Cindy moaned.

Adam was grim. "I had figured as much myself."

Sally smiled. "How was the police station? Did you get lots of help?"

Adam shrugged. "You were right. Don't rub it in." He gestured to the flamethrowers. "Does Mr. Patton have only two of them?"

"He has three but he's keeping one for himself," Sally said. "We can't complain. He gave us the easy payment plan on these two."

"He actually believed the story about the Cold People?" Cindy asked.

"He'll believe any story about any kind of secret attack," Bum said. "It's what he lives for."

Cindy checked her watch and grimaced. "It's already two o'clock. Watch was taken at noon. I hope he's all right."

"You heard what Bum said," Sally snapped. "We can't keep hoping he's fine. If we see him, we can't trust him. He's the enemy now."

Cindy was shocked. "How can you talk that way about our friend? I still have hope, and I will keep hoping until this is all over. I don't care what anyone says."

Sally started to snap back, then paused and drew in a deep breath. She momentarily closed her eyes. A spasm of pain crossed her face.

"I'm sorry," she said softly. "I have hope too."

Adam had never heard Sally say she was sorry before.

He wasn't given a chance to think about the apology, though.

They heard a loud shout from the front of the store.

"They're coming!" Mr. Patton cried. "I see them down the road!"

As Bum had said, the army surplus store was not located in Spooksville proper, but on the outskirts. Between the store and the hills was nothing but a road and a grass field littered with clumps of bushes and rocks. As they rushed outside, they saw several blue-clad figures coming over the hills. Mr. Patton had correctly identified them as Cold People because they were moving both stiffly and rapidly. There were six that Adam could see, but he had a feeling there were another half dozen just behind them. He was relieved that Watch wasn't with the group of monsters.

But otherwise he was more scared than he had ever been in his life.

Even from far away, the Cold People's eyes shone with a strange light.

"What do we do now?" Adam whispered.

Mr. Patton shouldered his M16 and grenade launcher. "It's party time, guys. Get your flame-throwers ready. Let's head them off before they make it into town. It's our day to be heroes."

"Where's your flamethrower?" Adam asked.

"Inside the store," Mr. Patton said, marching forward toward the advancing enemy. "You can use it if you want. Just don't blow yourself up."

"Wait for us," Bum said. "We should attack together."

Mr. Patton waved him away. "They're already dead meat. I don't need backup."

Bum turned to Adam. "Get the other flamethrower. It's behind the counter. It's already fueled up. Hurry!"

Adam rushed inside and got the weapon. He was stunned by its weight. He had to drag it outside. He figured the gasoline alone in it weighed twenty pounds. The tip was already lit, and it appeared easy to operate. If he squeezed the trigger, the flame grew longer.

Adam stepped back outside just in time to see Mr. Patton raise his M16.

The surplus store owner took aim at the nearest one of the Cold People.

Which just happened to be a woman.

"Take this, you ice-sucking monster!" Mr. Patton screamed and fired.

He obviously didn't have the weapon on rapid fire. He fired off only one bullet. He was an excellent shot; the bullet struck the creature in the center of the chest. The round made an odd sound as it struck, like a bullet bouncing off a steel plate.

But it did not hurt her. There was no blood.

Not breaking stride, the creature kept coming. Yet the cold blue light in its eyes grew brighter. The shot had not hurt it but had angered it. Mr. Patton briefly lowered his weapon and shivered. He was two hundred feet away from Adam, but Adam could see he was stunned.

"Don't stand still!" Sally yelled. "It'll freeze you solid!"

Mr. Patton appeared to hear Sally. Quickly he raised his M16 again. This time he let the whole clip of bullets fire. The ammunition tore at the creature's blue suit, but still it did not stop. Mr. Patton began to back up, dazed. Again Sally shouted at him.

"Try your grenade launcher!" she said.

"I think he should get back here," Cindy said anxiously.

"We may already be trapped ourselves," Bum said. "Remember, we can't outrun them."

Mr. Patton turned and ran back toward them. But it was then that the cold woman decided to chase after him. It was as fast as the one who had grabbed Watch. A glance over his shoulder showed Mr. Patton that he would be caught before he could reach the store. Finally he took Sally's last piece of advice. Dropping to one knee, he raised the grenade launcher and took aim. To his credit, he kept his hands steady, something Adam doubted he would have been able to do with one of those monsters bearing down on him.

Mr. Patton fired the grenade.

His aim was perfect. The grenade hit the creature's right shoulder.

There was a flash of fire and a loud bang.

Its right arm was gone. Shattered splinters.

The gang howled in delight.

"They can be stopped!" Sally yelled.

But Sally spoke too soon. The creature had lost a limb but there was no blood. In fact the wound didn't even slow it down. Looking closer, Adam saw that the arm appeared to have cracked off the way it would have from an ice sculpture. Mr. Patton had not destroyed it. Adam suspected these creatures could keep coming with both their legs blown off. Certainly they'd never bleed to death.

They didn't have any blood.

The cold creature fell on Mr. Patton.

He dropped his weapons and screamed.

They didn't hang around to see what the creature did to him.

"Back in the store!" Bum yelled.

They raced to the surplus store and closed the door. They were in luck. The doors and windows not only had strong locks, but heavy metal gratings as well. They pulled the steel bars over and snapped them shut just as the whole group of Cold People reached the front door and started pounding on it.

The door held.

They were safe, for the moment.

But they were also trapped.

6

IN THE GLOOM OF THE SURPLUS STORE, they stared at one another, their faces pale with fear. The creatures outside continued to circle the building. They had cut off the power, and the lights were out. The pounding on the front door had stopped but Adam knew the next attack would be worse.

"What are we going to do?" Cindy whispered.

"We're not going to get out of here on foot," Bum said. "That's for sure. But we might not need to. Just before you guys showed up, Sally and me found a couple of hot air balloons in back. They must be from the First World War. They were carefully packaged. I bet they'll still work, if we can get them up on the roof and inflated."

"But they can't get us in here," Cindy said. "Maybe we should just stay here until help arrives."

Sally shook her head. "No one's coming to save us. And you have to notice they're not leaving. They'll get in here eventually."

Adam peered out a crack in the window. "I don't see Mr. Patton. What do you think they did to him?"

"It's better not to think about it," Bum said. "Come on, let's get the balloons out."

The boxes the balloons came in were massive. Actually, there were four boxes per balloon. The balloon gondola and supporting ropes were packaged separately. There was also the wide-mouthed burner that went beneath the balloons, and which would allow them to control their height. At the moment Adam just wanted to get into a balloon and fly away as far as possible.

But he was worried about his family: his mother and father and little sister. He wished he could call them to warn them to get out of town, but the Cold People had destroyed the telephone lines. He prayed they weren't changed into monsters, although his little sister had been practicing to be a monster since her second birthday.

They were fortunate that there were stairs that led up to the roof. Working together, they were able to get all the balloon boxes up there. They were also lucky that the exterior walls of the surplus store were relatively smooth. The Cold People who were prowling around outside wouldn't be able to climb the walls and get onto the roof.

Standing on the roof and looking down, Adam could see that the monsters were not giving up. Bum stood beside him as he scanned the area. There were maybe ten Cold People visible. But Adam suspected there were more than that already entering the town. Bum put his hand on Adam's shoulder.

"Sally and I can put the balloons together," he said. "Why don't you and Cindy go back down into the store and keep guard?"

"That sounds like a good idea," Adam said.

"Keep your flamethrowers ready."

Adam nodded. "Work fast. They're strong. They'll get in here eventually and they know it."

Sally worked better alone, and Cindy was happy to leave her and join Adam on guard duty. Actually, *happy* may have been a poor word to describe Cindy's state of mind. Adam had seen her scared before, but never like this. In their minds, they could both still hear Mr. Patton's screams. But there was no sight of him. Cindy stayed close to his side as they patrolled the narrow aisles of the store. The minutes crept by.

"There are so many explosives in here," Cindy whispered finally. "If they do break in and we have to use our flamethrowers, we'll probably blow ourselves up."

"We have to be careful," Adam agreed. He gestured to what looked like a box of dynamite. "How did Mr. Patton ever get this stuff? You'd think it would be illegal."

"Everything is legal in Spooksville," Cindy said weakly. The words seemed to choke in her throat. Her eyes filled with tears. Adam touched her side.

"What is it?" he asked.

She put her hand to her head. "I keep thinking of Watch. I wish he was here with us. I wish we could take him with us in our balloons."

Adam patted her on the back. "I keep thinking of him too."

Cindy wiped at her face. "You must think I'm acting like a sissy. I don't usually cry. But since I've been here in this town, it's been one crisis after another."

"Yeah. But at least you never get bored."

Cindy forced a smile. "That's true."

Again Adam gestured to the box of dynamite. "I think we should load some of this into our balloons. You never know when it may come in handy."

"Why? You saw that the grenade didn't even stop the cold creature."

Adam paused. "I know that. I just have this feeling—I can't explain it. I think we might want this dynamite later." Adam bent over and studied the boxes. "Here, there are fuses and detonators and everything. I want to haul some up onto the roof. Will you be all right down here for a few minutes?"

Cindy glanced uneasily around the shadows. "Don't be gone too long."

Adam was surprised when he got back up on the roof to see that Sally and Bum nearly had the balloons together. In reality there were not many parts to assemble. Bum even had one of them already filling with hot air. The burner was blasting away beneath the huge canopy as Adam walked over and set down his case of dynamite.

"We should be able to take off in a few minutes," Bum said.

"Good," Adam said. "I want to take these explosives with us."

Sally looked up from her work. She was hooking the ropes onto the balloon gondola that would carry at least two of them aloft.

"The more firepower the better," she said.

"How is it downstairs?" Bum asked.

Before Adam could answer, they heard Cindy scream. Adam realized he had left his flamethrower downstairs because he needed both hands free to lift the dynamite onto the roof. He raced toward the ladder. Bum and Sally started to follow but Adam stopped them.

"Finish getting the balloons ready!" he yelled. "I'll save Cindy!"

Adam hurried downstairs. It was darker in the store than it had been only minutes ago. He saw his flamethrower lying at the base of the ladder where he had left it. The tip was still spouting a short flame. He didn't see his friend, or hear her anymore.

"Cindy!" he called as he picked up the flame thrower.

Off to his left, in the direction of the back door, he heard glass break.

"Adam!" Cindy shouted.

Relieved she could still respond, Adam ran toward her.

In the rear of the store, he found Cindy guarding a door that was about to cave in. As he feared, the Cold People were bending back the metal security bars. There were a total of four of them, all working on the same door. One of them was already squeezing its head through the bars and reaching for the lock.

"Shoot it!" Adam yelled as he ran up.

"I can't!" Cindy cried. "I just can't burn someone!"

"If you don't they'll freeze you." Adam pushed her out of the way and raised his flamethrower. The cold man took one look at the burning tip of the weapon and started to withdraw his head. Adam shot off a huge tongue of fire but it missed completely—the cold creature was that fast. But the wood around the door caught fire, which was not good because it made it easier for the door to collapse. Adam grabbed Cindy's hand. "We have to get out of here!" he said.

They ran toward the stairs that led up to the roof. But just as Cindy put her foot on the first rung, the back door exploded in a shower of sharp glass and twisted metal. All four Cold People rushed in. They came at Adam like flying blocks of ice. He shoved Cindy in the back.

"Get up on the roof!" he shouted.

"You come too!" Cindy cried.

"Give me a second," Adam said. With Cindy running up the stairs, he raised the flamethrower and squeezed the trigger hard. The stream of flame that flew out was huge—it caused the Cold People to scatter. But while they did, another two monsters burst in through the ruined back door. Adam realized he couldn't hold them off forever. He stepped onto the stairs and started up the steps.

He had almost made it to the roof when something cold grabbed his right ankle.

Adam tripped and fell.

Sprawled along the steps, he turned back and saw a creature below him.

Blue, icelike fingers were wrapped around Adam's foot.

The creature tightened its grip.

Adam felt its nails dig into his skin.

He saw blood—his blood. It stained his white socks red.

Adam gasped and raised his flamethrower. But he could not shoot the monster straight in the face, not unless he wanted to fry his own foot. For a second he didn't know what to do. Blood continued to stain his sock.

The creature began to pull him down.

Its eyes shone with cold light.

Adam decided he could stand a little burn.

He fired with the flamethrower. But he aimed high, above the creature's head and away from his bleeding foot. The heat of the fire, however, was enough to force the monster to jerk back a step. Adam was able to pull his foot free. But the monster was quick to recover. Once more it reached out with its freezing claw. But this time Adam was ready for it.

He shot the monster right in the face.

For a second the creature's head was a ball of pure flame.

Adam heard a weird scream. It was thin and high-pitched, the sound an alien bat might make as it died. Perhaps the Cold People were like evil vampires, Adam thought, who spread by stealing human blood and replacing it with Cryo fluid. The scream pierced Adam's chest and made his heart shiver.

But the monster's face did not burn.

Rather, it seemed to blur. Its features ran together. It was a ball of wax thrown into a simmering oven. The eyes seeped into the nose. The mouth dissolved into the chin. Its powerful hands seemed to reach up to hold the parts in place, but the moment they entered the flames, they too began to melt. Adam watched in horror and amazement. The creature toppled backward, and fell down the stairs.

It landed in a disfigured pile on the floor.

The other Cryo Creatures gathered around.

They stared down at their partner.

Then up at Adam. Their eyes *very* cold.

Adam felt hands on him, trying to pull him up onto the roof.

"We're ready to take off!" Sally yelled. "Leave them!"

"I'm coming," Adam said as he limped up the remainder of the steps.

But once on the roof, rather than running toward the waiting balloons, Adam turned back to the door and locked the flamethrower trigger on high. It was a shame to leave the weapon behind, but he was determined to even up the score for what they had done to Watch. With the weapon gushing fire, he threw it down into the store. The creatures scattered as it landed beside their fallen comrade. Adam noted the direction of the spouting flame.

It was pointed toward Mr. Patton's ammunition supplies.

Adam ran toward one of the waiting balloons.

He heard loud explosions below.

Adam limped as he ran.

His injured ankle was turning strangely numb.

7

ADAM ENDED UP IN THE BALLOON WITH SALLY.
Cindy was with Bum. They floated off the roof and were
dragged away from the surplus store by a gust of north
wind. Their escape came none too soon. Two Cryo
Creatures piled onto the roof. One leapt to catch Adam
and Sally's balloon, and barely missed. Sally hung over
the side and shot at it with her flamethrower.

"Just so it doesn't think of trying again," she said. She
had missed.

"They're not safe on that roof," Adam muttered.

"What do you mean?" Sally asked.

"Just watch," Adam said.

The grand finale came quickly. The two monsters

were trying to climb back down into the store when a river of flame shot up at them, and they were turned into melting torches. They staggered around the roof before toppling over the sides. There followed a series of crushing bangs and the entire rear of the store disintegrated. As one creature tried to run out the front door, there was a single massive explosion, and the store was engulfed in flame. Mr. Patton may not have sold too many exotic weapons in his day, but the weapons had done the job when they were needed.

"I think you got them all," Sally said.

Adam shook his head and slumped to the floor of the balloon gondola. He rubbed his right ankle. The wound was superficial; the bleeding had stopped. But he didn't seem to be able to get the circulation going in it.

"We got maybe eight of them," he said. "I think there are dozens more."

Sally noticed his bloody sock and knelt beside him. "Are you hurt? Are you in pain?"

"No. The creature barely dug his nails in. But—"

"What?" Sally asked.

"I don't know. My foot's numb. I can hardly stand on it."

Sally drew back anxiously. "Maybe when it grabbed you it injected Cryo fluid into your system. Maybe its going to circulate throughout your body and transform you into one of those horrible monsters. Soon you will start frothing at the mouth and crave human blood."

"Thank you, Sally," Adam said flatly. "You have an amazing way of making a guy feel good when things are not going well. I suppose now you want to change places with Cindy in the other balloon?"

"Well," Sally said.

"I'll throw you overboard if you don't stop," Adam warned.

Sally moved to his side and squeezed the flesh above his ankle. "Don't worry, I won't leave you. Can you feel that?"

"Yes. Sort of. I feel like . . ." Adam trailed off.

"The numb sensation is going up your leg?" Sally asked.

Adam hesitated. "Yes."

Sally looked worried. "We need to get you to a doctor."

"The only doctor who could help me lived back in Mu." Adam paused and swallowed thickly. He had to face the reality of the situation. "I might need to have my lower leg amputated. Before it spreads all the way up my body."

"In this town you don't need a doctor for that. Just

get down to the jetty and hang your leg in the water. A shark will bite it off for you."

Adam hung his head. "Thanks a lot. You wouldn't say that if it was your leg."

Sally leaned over and hugged him. "You know I really am worried. But maybe it's not as bad as it seems. Maybe the numbing sensation will wear off."

"I hope so," Adam said quietly.

"Hey, what's going on over there?" Cindy called from the other balloon, which was floating even with them, thirty feet away. Sally stood up to answer.

"None of your business," she called.

"Where's Adam?" Bum asked.

Sally glanced down at him. "He's resting. He's had a hard day." She added, "But don't worry. He's not turning into a monster."

Cindy and Bum looked at each other.

"Adam," Cindy said. "Are you sure you're all right?"

Adam struggled to his feet. "Yeah. I just twisted my ankle is all."

"He doesn't have a strange infection or anything," Sally said.

"Would you shut up," Adam whispered to her.

"What?" Sally whispered back. "I'm not saying anything."

"The day you don't say anything, the sky will crack open and angels will appear."

"That happened here once," Sally said.

"What do we do now?" Cindy called over.

Adam stared in the direction of town. They appeared to be drifting that way. He didn't see any more Cold People but he realized that meant nothing.

"Right now we're at the mercy of the wind," Adam called back. "At least it decides which way we're going. But using the burner we can rise high or sink lower. If we fly over some Cold People we might want to drop down and try to stop them with our flamethrowers."

"But soon people in town will be changed," Bum warned them. "Are we going to attack them as well?"

"There are some people in town I wouldn't mind melting," Sally muttered.

"We'll cross that bridge when we come to it," Adam said.

They didn't exactly come to a bridge, but they did drift toward the cemetery and Ann Templeton's castle. Even from a distance they could see there was a lot going on there. As they drew closer, they saw over a dozen Cold People circling the witch's home. The Cold People seemed to be laying siege to the place. Perhaps they knew of Ann's great powers. She had withdrawn the bridge that crossed her moat. Through the surrounding trees, Adam could just make out strange creatures loyal to Ms. Templeton guarding the walls and windows of the castle. The Cold People appeared to be trying to lay a huge fallen tree across the moat to invade the place. Over in the other balloon, Bum laughed at their efforts.

"They're not going to get to her," Bum said. "I'd bet everything I own on it."

"Yeah, but you're a bum," Sally said. "You don't own anything."

"Just watch," Bum said. "She'll give them a scare."

Bum knew his witch. Just as the Cold People toppled the tree across the moat and started to climb aboard, a bright flash of fire stabbed down from the top tower of the castle. There was a loud cracking sound, like lightning striking. The tree burst into fire and several of the Cold People were plunged into the water.

"There are crocodiles in that moat," Bum said.

Again he was right. As they watched, the Cold People in the water were attacked from below. Sally let out a cheer.

"They're falling faster than we thought they would!" she said.

But she spoke too soon. A couple of Cold People sank beneath the surface, but bobbed quickly back up.

And in their hands they each held a crocodile. The gang watched in horror as the cold monsters snapped the huge reptiles in half.

"I can't believe this," Cindy cried.

Another blast of fire shot down from the high tower. It hit the water and there was an explosion of steam. The Cold People retreated up the wall of the moat, away from the castle. They had been driven off, but none of them was destroyed.

"They might not be able to get to the witch," Adam said for all of them. "But she can't get out of her castle."

Bum agreed. "I think this is one battle we'll have to fight without her help." Bum stopped and peered into the cemetery, which was now directly below them. He pointed at a tombstone in the corner of the graveyard. He spoke with excitement. "Is that Watch?"

8

IT WAS DEFINITELY THEIR FRIEND.

Watch seemed dazed. He was wandering among the tombstones as if looking for his own grave. His clothes were slightly torn—mainly around the collar and at the hem of his pants. But he still had on his four watches and his thick glasses. He didn't seem to notice them, although they weren't far above, maybe only a hundred feet. Adam couldn't help noticing how pale his friend's skin was.

"We have to save him," Cindy called softly.

"That may not be a good idea," Bum said. "He might be beyond saving."

Sally turned to Adam. "What do you want to do?" she asked gently.

Adam felt choked with sorrow. "I sure don't want to leave him down there with all those monsters. But—"

"Yeah?" Sally said. "But what?"

Adam shook his head. "You know the situation. What do you think?"

Sally peered down into the cemetery. Watch had stopped and was just staring off into space. His eyes, seen through his thick glasses, appeared normal. But he was not standing as he usually did.

"There's something wrong with him," Sally said finally.

"I don't care," Cindy said. "He's still our friend. We can't abandon him."

"Not so loud," Sally warned. "He might hear us."

"We might want to call down to him," Bum said. "See how he reacts."

"No," Adam said. "If we shout to him, the other Cold People might hear too. At least right now, if we want to rescue him, he's alone."

"It's risky," Bum said. "We don't know how strong he is now. He could destroy us all."

Adam was grim. "Yeah. And we can't use our flame-throwers on him."

"But if he's changed," Sally said, "he might not know that we used to be his friends. He won't know that we won't try to fry him. If we surround him, we might be able to knock him out and then tie him up. We have extra rope."

"We're not going to hurt him," Cindy said.

"We might have to hurt him a little to help him," Sally snapped at her. "This is an emergency. Stop behaving like a little princess. We have to harden our hearts."

"If it was you I wouldn't mind picking up a bat," Cindy said.

"You would just end up clobbering yourself," Sally said.

"All right, all right," Adam said, wanting to stop them from arguing. "We'll drop down to see how he is. If he attacks, we'll try to knock him unconscious."

"If we take him with us," Bum said, "what are we going to do when he regains consciousness?"

"We'll worry about that later," Adam said.

"That's what the scientists who built the first atomic bomb would say to each other when someone asked 'What if we blow up the world?'" Sally muttered.

Dropping down was easy. All they had to do was vent off some of their hot air. Watch continued to stand staring off into space. Because the castle was next to the cemetery, the other Cold People were not far away, about a quarter of a mile. It would take a miracle for them not to see the balloons. For that reason Adam knew they had to act fast. He worried that they might be making a huge mistake. But he figured if he had to risk his life, it should be for his friend.

They landed in a small clearing in the cemetery, a hundred yards behind Watch's back. Still, incredibly, he appeared unaware of them. They had two flamethrowers left. Sally took one, Bum the other as they climbed out of the gondolas. Adam searched the ground for a strong stick, and found one that fit his grip.

But Adam limped as he walked.

The numbing sensation was definitely climbing.

As a group, they approached Watch.

Watch continued to stand gazing at a huge tombstone.

Adam realized it was Madeline Templeton's.

The tomb was the end of the Secret Path.

A portal into other dimensions.

Was Watch in such pain, Adam wondered, that he was thinking of fleeing into another reality? It was horrible to think of his friend possessed with the evil spirit of the Cryo Creatures.

But it was not as horrible as having to stare into his friend's face.

Watch suddenly whirled on them.

His eyes shone with a cold light.

His mouth twisted into an evil line.

A painfully high-pitched wail tore past his lips.

Then he attacked.

Adam—although lame—was leading the group and was therefore closest to Watch. He was the first one to suffer the brunt of Watch's newfound power. With his bad foot, he just couldn't move fast enough to get out of Watch's way. He felt as if he had been rammed by a freight train when Watch crashed into him. For a second Adam went flying through the air. He dropped his stick. He only stopped when he ran into a bigger stick—a tree, actually. It hurt to smash into the trunk, but Adam was back up in an instant.

The situation was already desperate and the fight was only three seconds old. As Adam's vision cleared, he saw that Cindy had also been knocked down. She may have been hit harder than he had because she didn't get up right away. Bum and Sally were still safe, for the moment, behind their flamethrowers. But they were doing nothing to corner Watch. On the contrary, Watch was driving them farther apart. Because they wouldn't fire, they had only the tiny flames at the tips of their flame throwers to scare him. Watch didn't look all that scared.

"Shoot off more fire," Adam said. "Let him know he can be burned."

"Good idea," Sally agreed, as she pulled back on her trigger. The tongue of flame stretched out three feet, and Watch quickly withdrew from attacking her. He turned to Bum instead, who had also lengthened his flame. Watch took a step back. Adam grabbed the stick he had dropped and limped forward.

"Drive him against the wall," Adam said. "We can only capture him if we corner him."

"Do we want to capture him?" Bum asked as he pushed Watch back with the flame. "We won't be able to control him."

"We can do what Sally said," Adam replied. "We can tie him up."

"I don't know if rope can hold him," Sally said, having second thoughts.

"Just get him against the wall," Adam ordered.

The wall surrounding the cemetery was high and nearby. A minute after they started on the offensive, Watch was cornered. He glared at them with his weird glowing eyes, and they each felt a chill. But he didn't have the power of an original Cryo Creature. He could make them shiver, but he couldn't freeze them.

"Now what?" Sally demanded.

"Now I'll talk to him," Adam said, taking a wobbly step forward.

"What are you going to talk about?" Sally asked. "Ice cream? Popsicles? Smoothies? The guy is a walking ice cube. You can't talk to him."

Adam gripped his stick tightly. "A part of him must remember us."

"We'll keep guard," Bum said. "But if he does attack, we may have to burn him a little."

"I understand," Adam said. "Try not to burn me while you're at it."

Adam stepped to within ten feet of Watch. His friend had his back pressed against the wall. He continued to glare at them, although something in his eyes seemed to change as he stared at Adam. There may have been a flicker of recognition. Adam couldn't be sure, but it gave him hope.

"Watch," Adam said. "We don't want to hurt you. We want to help you. Do you remember me, Watch? I'm Adam. I'm your friend."

Watch stopped glaring and his right cheek twitched. The weird light in his eyes faded, although his eyes did not return to normal. There was a blankness to them that Adam found disturbing. It was as if Watch's brain had been wiped clean by the cold man. Once again Adam wondered if Watch could ever be returned to normal.

"I really am your friend, Watch," Adam said,

encouraged by the change, any change, in his condi-
tion. Adam took another step forward and held out his
hand. "You can come with us. We'll take you away from
these evil monsters."

At the mention of the word *monsters* Watch glanced
in the direction of the castle. So far the other Cold
People had not appeared. But Adam knew their luck
couldn't last forever. Watch's dull expression trembled
as he looked in the direction of his new partners. For a
moment he appeared terribly sad. Adam took another
step toward him. Watch was now only five feet away.

"Please try to remember," Adam pleaded. "Your name
is Watch. You're a human being."

For a second Watch's dull expression vanished.

He smiled faintly. Adam smiled brightly.

"Watch!" Adam cried. He dropped his stick and
moved to hug his friend.

But the smile faded. The cold light returned.

Watch leapt toward Adam, his fingers spread like
claws.

Again, Adam felt a terrible blow and went down.
Through a fog of physical and emotional pain, he saw
Watch raise his claws to rip into his chest and pull out
his heart and fill his body with Cryo fluid. But before
Watch could strike again, Adam also saw the blur of

a brown stick as it was brought down on the back of Watch's head. His friend blinked and the wicked light in his eyes went out. Watch toppled aside.

"He has a hard head," Sally said, setting aside the stick Adam had dropped. Adam noticed that the stick was broken in half. Sally must have hit Watch pretty hard. He lay sprawled on his back. He didn't appear to be breathing. Adam knelt anxiously by his side.

"Is he dead?" he moaned.

Bum shook his head. "Cryo Creatures don't breathe. I don't even know if their hearts beat."

"Is he all right?" Cindy called, staggering over, a hand to her head.

"He's unconscious," Adam said. "But we think he's alive. How are you?"

"She looks terrible," Sally muttered.

Cindy snorted in Sally's direction. "You get hit the way I was and we'll see how long you stay down." She nodded to Watch. "Let's get him into one of the balloons."

"I don't like this," Bum said as he leaned over to pick up Watch. "But if we're going to take him, we better take him now." He nodded in the direction of the castle. "I think they heard us. They're coming."

Bum was right—four of the Cold People were

climbing the cemetery walls. The monsters had three times as far to go to get to the balloons, but Adam wondered who was going to get there first. His leg seemed to be getting worse with each passing second. It was now almost completely numb, and the cold sensation was as high up as his right knee. He fell behind the others as they raced for the balloons. He wondered if he would be joining Watch as a monster soon.

Sally reached the balloons first, of course, and began to loosen the ropes that would allow them to take off.

"Hurry!" Sally screamed. "Adam!"

Cindy arrived next, followed by Bum carrying Watch. But Adam was now tripping every other step. As he climbed back up, he saw that he was already too late. One of the Cold People had moved between him and the balloons. He was trapped, in a cemetery more dangerous than a snake pit. Adam froze as the cold person fixed him with its gaze and slowly began to approach.

"Get away!" he called to the others. "Save yourselves!"

"Drop that hero garbage!" Sally called back, climbing out of her balloon with her flamethrower ready. So intent was the creature on Adam that it hardly seemed to notice Sally.

Until Sally torched it from behind.

Like the one in the surplus store, the creature did not burn. It was more like it melted into a pile of blue fluid. Sally kept the flame blazing until there was nothing left except a smelly puddle sitting atop a grave. Sally grabbed Adam by the arm and pulled him toward one of the balloons.

"I just hope I never have to do that to Watch," she said, adding, "or to you."

9

THEY FLOATED UP AND OUT OF THE CEMETERY before any more Cold People could get them. Adam was with Sally and Watch. Their friend lay sprawled on his back on the floor of the gondola. Sally knelt at Watch's feet, tying his ankles together. Adam sat on the floor of the gondola as well. He didn't know if he could stand without support. The exercise in the cemetery had done nothing to drive away the numbness.

"I wish you didn't have to do that," Adam said to Sally.

She began to knot the rope. "Just wait till he wakes up and we'll see what you wish."

Adam put his hand on top of Watch's head.

It was like touching a block of ice.

"It's like he's dead," Adam said.

"Maybe it would be better if he were."

Adam was shocked. "How can you say that?"

Sally lowered her head. "I just have to look at him. He's not Watch anymore."

"But you saw him just before he attacked. For a second he recognized me."

Sally nodded sadly. "I saw it. I hope it means something." She sighed and stood and looked out over the city. "We're drifting toward the center of town. I think I see more Cold People below us."

Adam clawed his way up and leaned against the side. He was stunned to see three Cold People run into a house directly below them and drag a man and woman out onto the lawn. The Cold People pinned the couple to the grass. Adam had to look away. He could not bear to see how the monsters made more of themselves.

"We can't just float around up here all day," he said. "We have to take more aggressive action."

Sally sat beside him. "We're probably not going to get another situation like we had at the surplus store where we were able to get a bunch of them at once. I think the best we can do is swoop down every now and then and get one or two of them."

"That's no good," Adam said. "Especially since they're

making more of their kind every few minutes. We have to do something that will wipe them all out at once." Adam pounded his numb leg lightly with his clenched fist. "What is it that they're afraid of besides fire?"

Sally was thoughtful. "We haven't seen anything else. We know bullets and grenades can't stop them."

A remarkable idea occurred to Adam. "Wait a second! We asked ourselves earlier why they appeared today. We thought the cold weather had something to do with it."

"Yeah. We guessed that they might even have changed the weather."

"Yes, exactly," Adam said. "They probably did. It's summer and it's freezing today. That's an incredible coincidence. But what we didn't ask ourselves is *why* they would have changed the weather."

Sally shrugged. "They probably like the cold."

"No," Adam said. "They probably *need* the cold. There's a big difference between liking something and needing it. I wonder if it got warmer if they would all begin to die. Remember Bum's story. When Atlantis attacked Mu, the Cryo Creatures dashed up to the North Pole."

"So they wouldn't be killed by the nuclear blasts," Sally said.

"If they were just worried about the blasts, they could

have gone anywhere else. But they didn't go anywhere else. I think they fled to the North Pole because all the bombs—and the asteroid—raised the temperature of the whole world. It's possible they *had* to go to the North Pole."

"What's your point?" Sally asked. "We don't have any nuclear bombs here. Or asteroids. We can't just change the weather."

Adam sat up straighter. He could feel the power of his idea. He was sure he was onto something important.

"A couple of weeks ago we were having an argument about the witch," he said. "You were complaining about how rich she was, and how she never shared her wealth. You also said she was wrecking the local environment. Do you remember?"

"Yes. So what?"

"You said the worst thing she ever did—besides murdering hundreds of innocent children—was drill several huge oil wells in the hills behind Spooksville. You said they were somewhere above the reservoir."

Sally paused. "What are you saying?"

"The reservoir supplies the water for all of Spooksville. It also has many underground streams that lead away from it and flow under the entire city. We've heard the streams before when we've been up there. When we were trapped in the Haunted Cave, we even saw one of those streams."

"Say what you have to say. You're driving me crazy."

"Don't you see?" Adam said. "If we can divert the oil that's being pumped out of the ground at the witch's wells, we can flood the reservoir with tons of oil. And if we're able to ignite that oil, we will have the biggest fire this area has seen in the last ten thousand years. The local temperature will soar."

"Up in the hills," Sally protested. "Not so much down here."

"You're wrong. You're forgetting what I said about the underground streams. The water in them will heat as well. It will boil, and it will heat the ground. If we can get enough oil, if we can cause the whole reservoir to burn, we can drive the temperature back up."

Sally considered for a long time. "It's not easy to ignite crude oil that's been mixed with water. You need something powerful to trigger the fuel."

Adam patted the box of dynamite that rested beside them. "What do you think I brought this for?"

Sally was amazed. "You didn't have this idea back at the surplus store?"

Adam shook his head. "No. I just had this feeling—I can't explain it. Maybe there is such a thing as intuition."

Sally nodded. "I like this plan. I like big fires. But we're going to have trouble making it all work. The wind decides the course of this balloon. We're going to have to land, and we're going to need transportation up to the hills—fast transportation." Sally paused. "We need a Jeep. Something that can climb through hills."

"But we don't know how to drive."

"Speak for yourself. I learned to drive in kindergarten."

"But you don't have a driver's license," Adam said.

"I think that's the least of our worries right now." Sally gestured to Watch. "We shouldn't take him with us. He might ruin the whole plan."

"I don't want to leave him helpless while all that trouble is going on below us."

"I understand," Sally said. "But if we do get a Jeep, we're locking him in the trunk."

"Do Jeeps have trunks?" Adam asked.

"We'll find one that does." Sally stood. "We need to tell the others about our plan."

"You can tell them you thought it up if you like."

"I was going to do that anyway," she replied.

10

THEY DIDN'T SPOT A JEEP, BUT FOUND A large four-wheel-drive truck with a camper shell on the back. They decided not to be choosy. The city below was turning to chaos. The Cold People had invaded the local shopping center. People were running and screaming everywhere. Plus Adam and Sally now began to see a new horror. Many of the people the Cryo Creatures had first changed were already going after those who had not been changed. Adam figured by sunset it would be all over, at least for Spooksville.

Unless his plan worked.

On the floor of the gondola, Watch continued to lie still.

"I wish some of these panicking people would light a few fires," Sally said as they began to descend toward the track. "They don't know anything about rioting."

"It's not a skill you can practice," Adam said.

"How are you going to start the truck without keys?" Cindy called from the other balloon, which was descending as well. Cindy and Bum would stand guard while Watch and the dynamite were moved into the truck.

"I'm going to hot-wire it," Sally said.

"Who taught you how to do that?" Adam asked.

"I did," Bum said. "You never know when the skill will come in handy." He added, "Like right now."

"How are you going to get into the truck without keys?" Cindy asked.

"What are all these stupid questions?" Sally snapped impatiently. "We're trying to save the world here, Cindy, in case you didn't notice. I will take a big rock and break the window if I have to."

"I was just asking," Cindy muttered.

"You might want to land on top of the truck," Bum said. "It will give you some protection."

"I was thinking the same thing," Adam replied. Although the balloon could not really be steered, it could be maneuvered slightly by tightening and loosening the ropes that supported the balloon itself. Adam had already lowered the burner and vented a lot of hot air. They were going down pretty fast. The street the truck was parked on looked like a war zone.

Adam was barely able to hold himself up by hanging on to the side of the gondola. His right leg was completely numb up to midthigh. He wouldn't be able to walk without hanging on to Sally. He wouldn't be able to transfer the dynamite or move Watch. Sally would have to do everything. He hated feeling so helpless.

"I really think you guys should take Watch," Sally said when they were only twenty feet above the truck. "We don't need anything to slow us down."

"We'd both have to land to transfer him," Bum said. "That could be dangerous."

"It might not be a good idea to move him while he's unconscious," Cindy added.

Sally snorted and spoke to Adam. "They just don't want him. They're afraid of him. Oh well, I guess you learn who your friends really are when you've been transformed into a monster."

"You know, you've been a pain all day," Cindy said.

Sally laughed. "I am one of mankind's last hopes for salvation. I have the right to be a pain."

Cindy looked at Bum.

"She does have a point there," Bum said.

"Get ready," Adam said. "We're directly above the truck. I'm going to dump another bunch of hot air. We'll drop like a rock."

They didn't exactly drop like rock, but they came down hard. Watch seemed to stir as a result of the jolt. Adam was the only one to notice. Sally was already out of the gondola and trying to break into the car. It was Adam's turn to hold the flame thrower. If a Cryo Creature so much as looked their way, he was turning up the heat.

Cindy and Bum floated twenty feet overhead.

"Make sure you have gas in the truck," Bum called down. "It's a long drive up to the wells."

"I hope we don't have to stop for service," Sally called back. She had tried the door and it was locked. Picking up a nearby brick, she smashed the driver's window and reached in and tripped the lock. After opening the door, she tried to brush away the little pieces of glass. She would probably cut her butt on the way up to the hills. Just what she needed.

Adam handed her the case of dynamite as she jumped back on top of the truck. She had no problem loading it on to the front seat of the truck. But when she returned for Watch and Adam, she wondered how she was going to help them into the truck.

"You won't be able to lift Watch over the side of the gondola," Adam said. "And I won't be able to help you lift him. So what we're going to have to do is burn a hole in the side of it. Then you can just pull Watch out and slide him down." Adam gestured for her to stand back. "I'll try not to start a major fire."

Adam half-kept his promise. He blasted away a large chunk of the gondola and Sally was able to slide Watch out and stuff him into the truck's camper. She locked him inside, in fact. Unfortunately, the gondola continued to burn and the flames went into the balloon itself. Adam was barely clear before the hot air caused by the fire shot the balloon into the sky.

It flew right by Bum and Cindy, before self-destructing in a ball of flame.

"I hate to see it go," Sally said to Adam as she helped him into the passenger side. "It saved our lives a couple of times."

"When all this is over we'll go for a real hot air balloon ride," Adam said. He dragged his lifeless leg into the truck and shut the door and rolled down the window. Cradling the flame thrower on his lap, he leaned out the window and signaled to Cindy and Bum to get away. "Try to help people where you can," he called.

Bum shook his head. "You guys are our only hope."

"Good luck!" Cindy called.

"Bless you!" Sally called back sarcastically before climbing in the truck. She took one look at the truck's gears and groaned. "Oh no."

"What's the matter?" Adam asked, the box of dynamite sitting between them.

"It's a stick shift. I learned on an automatic."

"What's the difference?"

"What do you mean what's the difference? I know how to drive one type. I don't know how to drive the other."

"Well, you're just going to have to learn," Adam said.

"That's easy for you to say. How come you don't know how to drive?"

"Because I'm twelve years old and I'm originally from a normal town in the Midwest where they don't teach twelve-year-olds to drive. Now would you quit complaining and just get us out of here. This street isn't exactly safe, in case you hadn't noticed."

"I'll try. That's all a girl can do." Sally pulled up the seat so her feet could reach the pedals. It was fortunate that Sally's legs were as long as they were, or else they would have had to steal a motorcycle. Next she lifted up the brick she had used to smash the window. Bringing it down on the ignition switch—and breaking it—she pulled out a couple of red and yellow wires. When she touched them together the engine roared to life and the truck leapt forward.

Then the engine stalled.

"Why did that happen?" Adam demanded. "Are we out of gas?"

"No. I think I need to start with the truck in neutral."

"Then do that," Adam snapped.

"I am! I just happen to be going through a tough learning curve right now. Give me a second." Sally pressed in one of the pedals on the floor and shifted the gears into the N position. Again she touched the wires together. The engine started and the truck began to roll forward. Sally shifted the gears once more—this time to 1—and the truck picked up speed. "I'm a genius!" Sally exclaimed.

They ran into a fire hydrant.

The water exploded like a geyser.

It drenched their hood. They could have been in a storm.

"What kind of genius are you?" Adam asked.

"The kind that doesn't respond well to criticism." Sally shifted into reverse. "Fasten your seat belt and don't say another word."

11

TEN MINUTES AFTER SAYING GOOD-BYE TO
Adam and Sally, Cindy and Bum began to feel guilty
about not doing more to help their friends. At least
Cindy felt guilty. She didn't know if guilt was an emo-
tion Bum allowed himself to experience.

"Maybe we should have gone with them," she
said as they floated toward the beach. The invasion
was sweeping the whole town. Cindy kept putting
her hands over her ears and eyes. But she could not
block out what was happening. What she wanted to
do more than anything in the whole world was rescue
her mother and her younger brother, Neil. But she
wondered if it was a selfish thought. Bum had said it

right. Their real hope lay with Adam and Sally.

"I don't know if we could have helped them that way," Bum said.

"But we're not doing anybody any good up here," Cindy protested.

Bum gestured. "Will we do any good getting changed into Cryo creatures?"

Cindy searched for the ruined lighthouse, which was not far from her home. But they were at least two miles north of her street. If they landed, and she did manage to fight through to her house and reach her mother and brother, the balloon would surely not be there when she got back.

"I wish we'd found a helicopter in the surplus store," she said, frustrated. "Not being able to steer this thing is driving me crazy."

Bum scratched his unshaven face. "I've been thinking about that very problem. There might be a solution. Coming up below us is a hardware store. You can see it there beside those trees. They carry large fans. We might be able to rig one up and use it for propulsion and steering."

"What would we use to power it? We can't plug it in."

"There are portable generators in the store. They run on gasoline. We could drain some fuel out of our flamethrower. We wouldn't need much. The largest fan would only need a small generator to power it."

Cindy liked the idea. "Where would we head?"

Bum spoke gently. "I know you have family in town. We could try to rescue them." He added, "If that's what you want."

Cindy looked down at the madness. Several fires had broken out. Homes and cars were burning. To think of her mother and brother down there was too painful for Cindy.

"Let's get the fan and generator," she whispered. "Then we can decide."

Bum was becoming an expert at ballooning. He brought them down right on top of the hardware store. He anchored their flying machine by tying one of its ropes to a roof vent. He offered to let her carry the flamethrower but she declined.

"At the surplus store I found I couldn't burn anyone," she said.

"We were lucky Sally doesn't have your inhibitions," Bum said.

Cindy nodded. "She is brave, and I admire her for that." She added, "I just never tell her that."

They found a way into the hardware store attic. From there they had no trouble getting down to the main level. The place was deserted, and they supposed that was a good thing. But Cindy found the silent aisles spooky. She kept thinking something was going to jump out at them. Bum steered them in the direction of the fans.

"Look, they're on sale," Bum said as they reached the right department. "That's a big break. I haven't cashed my paycheck," he teased.

"How do you survive out on the streets without money?"

"I rely on my good looks and charm."

"No, really. I often wonder how you eat. Where you sleep."

Bum spoke seriously. "Cindy. Mankind has existed on this planet for centuries before the invention of money. Dollar bills and credit cards do not make the world go round, as most people think. I was rich at one time and now I'm poor. But I have to say I'm a lot happier owning nothing than owning tons of stuff I hadn't paid for. Does that make sense?"

Cindy chuckled. "It makes perfect sense."

They studied the fans, trying to figure out which one would be best. They ended up selecting two large round ones on stands. Choosing a generator was easy. There were only two types: a big one and a small one.

The big one was for powering heavy equipment. They took the small one.

They were loading the equipment up into the attic when they were attacked.

The creature came from nowhere.

He grabbed Bum from behind and lifted him off his feet.

Bum was squeezed tight.

He dropped the flamethrower. It clanged at his feet.

"Cindy!" Bum shouted. "Help!"

Cindy froze in terror when she saw what was happening. This creature did not wear a blue jump suit. This was not one of the original Cryo Creatures. Like Watch, this man had started out the day as a normal human being. But now he was the enemy. As Cindy stood stunned, the thing began to drag Bum away. It was strong. Bum fought and kicked but couldn't break loose.

"The flamethrower," Bum gasped as he was yanked around the corner. "Cindy."

By a sheer act of will, Cindy broke her paralysis. She grabbed the flamethrower and chased after Bum and the creature. For a man who had just been changed into a monster, he sure moved fast. She only caught up to them as the creature was about to drag Bum outside.

She raised the flamethrower, pulling back slightly on the trigger. The flame moved out a foot.

"Let go of him or you burn!" she shouted.

This creature wasn't totally stupid. It understood what fire was, and it knew that it could use Bum as a shield. It moved Bum between himself and the fire.

"What should I do?" Cindy cried. "I can't get off a clear shot."

Bum struggled. "On the count of three I'm going to yank forward and down as hard as I can. Aim for the top of his head. The heat might startle him. He might let me go. Ready? One. Two—"

"Wait!" Cindy cried.

"What is it?" Bum asked.

"I've never shot anyone before!"

"It's easy. Just pretend you're Sally."

"I don't see how anyone can be Sally. How can I pretend to be her?"

Bum groaned as the creature bent back his arms. "Then just close your eyes and pull the trigger when I get to three. I don't know how long I can hold out against this guy. Please, Cindy."

She nodded frantically. "Okay. Do it. Say it."

"One. Two. Three!"

Bum yanked forward and ducked his head. Cindy

took quick aim and fired. She didn't shoot directly at the man's face, but just above his head. She couldn't bear the thought that if somehow they could reverse the damage caused by the Cold People, this man would wake up tomorrow with a burnt face.

But Cindy's aim was not far off the creature's face.

She singed its hair.

The creature let go of Bum and turned and fled.

He ran out the door howling.

Bum staggered to Cindy's side.

He nodded as he took the flamethrower back.

"I'll tell Sally you wasted the guy," he said.

Cindy smiled. "Tell her there were ten of them."

They loaded their equipment into the balloon.

The fans and generator worked like a charm.

"What course?" Bum asked as they left the hardware store.

Cindy turned away from the direction of the lighthouse and her house. Like it or not, she realized, all of Spooksville was her home. She had to help save it all.

"Let's head for the hills," she said. "Let's help Adam and Sally."

12

ADAM WAS FEELING COLD ALL OVER. WORSE, he was having cold thoughts. As they roared out of town and into the hills, he kept looking over at Sally and thinking of all the warm blood in her veins. How he hated the fact that she was warm while he was cold.

How he wanted to make her cold, too.

Adam knew the sick thoughts were from his wound. He had to fight to keep them away.

He knew now he was slowly changing into a monster.

Sally glanced over at him. "Are you okay?"

He nodded. "Yeah. Just keep driving."

"You don't look okay. How's your leg?"

"It's okay."

"Can you feel it?" she asked.

"No."

"Then how can you say it's okay?"

"Would you just shut up and drive!" Adam snapped. He stopped himself, dragging in a ragged breath. "I'm sorry, Sally. I don't feel good. I feel cold. Could you please turn on the heater?"

"I have it all the way up. It's roasting in here. Has the numbing sensation spread?"

Adam smiled bitterly. "Yeah. It's spreading."

Spreading right into his brain.

He knew he didn't have much time left.

The four-wheel-drive truck was a wonderful machine. It allowed them not only to plow into the hills, but to keep going even when the road ran out. They blew past the reservoir at high speed. Just up ahead Adam could see the oil wells, bobbing up and down like giant insects. In the orange evening light, they looked ready to burn.

Soon the sun would set.

"Faster," Adam whispered.

Finally they reached the oil wells. There were six of them, clustered around a series of eight storage tanks. Adam realized the lines from the wells fed the tanks, and that it was the tanks they had to crack. The suckers were huge. If they could drain them dry, there would be enough oil to fill the reservoir. The oil would just pour down into the water. He explained his thoughts to Sally.

But he didn't tell her he couldn't stop thinking about how unfair it was that she was warm while he was shivering. He hoped the growing insanity did not show in his eyes.

"But we don't want to dynamite the tanks," Sally said. "They might catch fire. It's better that the oil goes into the reservoir."

Adam sucked in another breath and tried to steady his shivering body. "Take eight sticks of dynamite and cut off three-quarters of each. Keep the fuses intact." Adam had to struggle to get the words out. "Plant a partial stick beneath each line that leads into each tank. If we blow all the lines, the oil will gush out."

Sally watched him, worried. "You sound weird. Your voice—you don't sound like Adam."

He shook his head. "I am still Adam. Just do it. Do it fast. We don't have much time."

Sally reached out and touched his arm. But she withdrew her hand when she felt how cold he was. Her eyes were red; she was close to tears.

"Isn't there something I can do for you?" she begged.

Adam forced a smile. "Save the world, Sally. That's all you can do."

Sally took several dynamite sticks and walked to the storage tank lines. She carried a knife. Adam watched as she cut eight of the sticks down to a small size. Sally kept the flamethrower nearby.

She was planting them beneath the lines when Watch began to stir.

"Oh no," Adam groaned. "Just what we don't need."

Watch sat up in the back and peered in at Adam through the window that separated them.

In the evening gloom, his eyes glowed with evil light.

Adam was too weak to flee.

"Watch," Adam said gently. "Don't do anything weird right now. We're almost home. Just sit here quietly and everything will be all right."

Watch was not interested in his advice.

With one swift smash of his fist, Watch broke the glass. He reached in and grabbed Adam by the throat. Adam tried not to scream but he made some sound. He heard Sally scream and run toward them. Out of the corner of her eye he saw her raise the flamethrower. At the same time he felt Watch's cold breath on his cheek. He didn't know what his friend was going to do to him, but he imagined it was not going to be pleasant.

"Watch," Adam gasped. "You're my friend."

The words had some effect. Watch hesitated for a

second. As it had in the cemetery, the cold light in his eyes briefly faded. His blank expression contorted. It was as if he was trying to remember Adam from another life. Perhaps he would have remembered him, but Sally arrived right then, and Sally did not believe in reasoning with a monster.

"Let him go!" Sally shouted as she aimed the flame thrower at the camper portion of the truck. "Let him go or you're Liquid Drano!"

Watch released Adam and immediately turned on Sally. He did so by smashing through the side window of the camper and leaping outside. His speed was breathtaking. He stalked Sally but she kept him at a distance with her flamethrower. Yet she was not willing to burn him, and Watch seemed to know that now. He didn't seem to be as frightened of the fire as before.

And Sally had other problems.

Her flame seemed to shorten even as she pulled harder on the trigger.

"I'm running out of fuel!" she called to Adam.

"Back up in the direction of the dynamite sticks!" Adam shouted. "We must blow those lines and we must blow them now!"

"We still have to light the oil once it's in the reservoir!" Sally called. Keeping an eye and the flame on Watch, she managed to walk back to the tanks. There she broke into a jog, brushing each stick's fuse with her flame as she passed. It was a dangerous maneuver. If her aim was only slightly off, the dynamite would go off in her face.

But Sally had a steady hand.

Soon all the fuses were burning bright.

Still, Sally's flamethrower continued to fail. She tried getting back to Adam and the truck, but at each turn Watch blocked her way. Watch seemed particularly intent on getting to her. Perhaps he remembered how she had knocked him over the head in the cemetery.

"I can't reach you!" Sally cried.

"It doesn't matter," Adam called back. "Just get away from the oil lines."

Sally did as he told her, even as Watch continued to stalk her. "I can't hold him off much longer!"

"Listen," Adam called. "As the sticks explode, make a dash down the hill. I'll slip the truck into neutral. I'll pick you up as I coast by."

"But your leg is numb!" Sally shouted back. "You won't be able to brake!"

"I'll do the best I can," Adam said.

Ten seconds later the sticks began to explode. They went in a tight series, one after the other. The explosions seemed to check Watch. He froze—of course he was already frozen—and Sally had a chance to run down the hill toward the reservoir. She just dropped the flamethrower and split.

She was not the only thing that raced toward the reservoir.

As the last dynamite stick went off, Adam saw a large wave of oil chasing Sally. The line to each tank had ruptured. It was a black tidal wave. No question about it—the reservoir would be flooded with fuel.

Adam dragged himself into the driver's seat and released the parking brake. The truck began to coast down the hill, rapidly picking up speed. He was able to steer but by now both his legs were without feeling. Sally was right—he couldn't brake. By the time he reached her he was doing thirty miles an hour. There was no way she could leap onto the truck.

"Adam!" she yelled.

"Sorry!" he shouted back as he flew past.

Adam was able to keep from plunging into the water by turning sharply to the right just as he reached the bottom of the hill. His wild steering sent up a huge dust cloud. The sharp turn also took him out of the way of the approaching oil wave. Unfortunately, he had also put more distance between himself and Sally. Distance he couldn't make up by driving over and picking her up.

His legs refused to work. He couldn't put the car in gear to get it to move any farther.

He was stuck where he was.

He saw Sally reach the water just before Watch. But she had no flamethrower to ward him off. She didn't even have a good stick. She glanced desperately in his direction, and Adam could see the fear in her eyes— even from a hundred yards away.

"What should I do?" she screamed.

There was only one hope.

"Jump in the water!" Adam yelled. "Swim out to the middle of the reservoir!"

"But this water's poisonous! It makes your hair all funny!"

"Don't worry about that now! He's coming right toward you!"

Sally could see that she didn't have many options. Watch was now only thirty feet away and closing. Whirling, Sally dashed into the reservoir and began to swim frantically away from the shore. For a moment it seemed Watch would try to follow her. But like the creatures that fell in the witch's moat, he seemed uneasy about the water. Plus he could not stay where he was. The oil was close on his heels. Watch was forced to run to the side.

Luckily for Adam, he ran to the other side.

Now Adam had a wave of oil between him and Watch.

And Adam had to make the toughest decision of his life.

The oil was flooding the reservoir at an incredible rate. In just a few minutes he should be able to ignite the oil slick with the box of dynamite. The only trouble was Sally had to stay in the water to stay away from Watch, and if she did stay there she would burn. Sally could not even circle around to reach Adam. The oil slick had already come between him and her. Sally could only swim toward the center of the reservoir.

Adam could not kill her. He knew this.

But he could not let all of Spooksville die either.

He knew that as well.

He pulled the case of dynamite with him as he crawled out of the truck.

He had a Bic lighter. He just had to set the case next to the shore. The oil would reach him soon. He just had to set the fuse, light it, and crawl away. He could make the fuse as long as he liked. He could give Sally as many extra minutes as she asked for. The trouble was none of those minutes would be enough. Even if she could out-swim the growing slick to reach the other side, Watch would be waiting for her.

Adam couldn't believe how horrible the situation was.

And he was so cold. He couldn't stop shaking.

But he had hit rock bottom before.

He should have remembered that when things were at their worst, they usually got better.

Adam looked up and saw a balloon in the sky. Not just any balloon, but one carrying Cindy and Bum. His friends seemed to understand the situation because they were heading straight for Sally. Their balloon was powered by what looked like hardware store fans. They had speed and steering ability.

Sally saw them and waved her arms frantically.

The oil slick was closing in on her.

Adam broke open the case of dynamite and pulled out his longest fuse.

The oil slick was moving his way as well.

The balloon dipped low. Cindy reached over the edge.

Adam set his fuse and grabbed his Bic lighter.

Sally reached up and grabbed Cindy's hand.

The oil slick touched Sally's foot just as she was pulled up into the balloon.

The slick touched a crippled Adam just as he lit the fuse and began to crawl away from the water. Far across the black reservoir, Watch seemed to finally understand what they were trying to do. He let out a high-pitched howl.

But there was nothing he could do to stop them.

The balloon rose high into the sky.

Adam crawled clear of the oil.

The dynamite exploded. The reservoir caught fire.

It lit up the sky. It lit up the heavens.

The temperature began to climb. In the hills and in the city.

All over Spooksville, the original Cryo Creatures began to melt.

And those they had changed returned to normal.

Even Adam. The feeling returned to his whole body.

Even Watch. Who had not been normal to begin with.

Epilogue

WHEN IT WAS ALL OVER, AND THE FIRE HAD finally begun to die down, the gang rode the four-wheel-drive truck back to town. This time Bum drove. He didn't have a license either, but he seemed familiar with stick shifts. Cindy sat up front with Bum. Adam and Sally were in back with Watch.

The last thing Watch remembered was thawing out the block of ice.

He didn't even remember the cold man.

But he believed everything they told him. And he seemed unmoved by the fact he had almost killed all of them. Sally frowned at his lack of feeling on the matter.

"I think you're still a little cold," she said.

"I always have been," Watch agreed. "But what I still want to know is why these creatures showed up now? Who put them here?"

"I think that's a riddle for another day," Bum said from the front.

"I hope I never live to see the day those things return," Cindy said.

"Hey, let's look on the bright side," Adam said. "We had another incredible adventure and we came out winners. We should celebrate."

"Yeah," Watch said. "Let's go get some ice cream."

A silence fell over the truck.

None of them thought that was a good idea.

TURN THE PAGE FOR A SNEAK PEAK AT
SPOOKVILLE #6: THE WITCH'S REVENGE

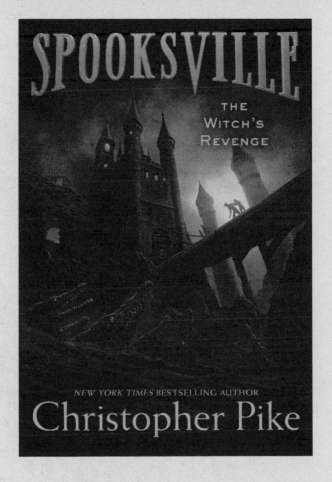

1

THE ARGUMENT WAS OLD. WAS MS. ANN Templeton, Spooksville's most powerful and beautiful resident, a good witch or a bad witch? There was no question that she was a *real* witch. Adam Freeman and his friends had seen too many demonstrations of her power to doubt that. But whereas Adam and Watch liked to think she was a nice person, Sally Wilcox and Cindy Makey were certain she was dangerous.

The argument started in the Frozen Cow, Spooksville's best-known ice-cream parlor. Because the owner would serve only vanilla ice cream, they were each having a vanilla shake when the idea of visiting the witch's castle came up. Of course later they would blame each other for the idea. Later, that is, when they couldn't find their way out of the castle.

It was a hot summer Wednesday, ten in the morning, a perfect time for a milk shake. School was still a few weeks away. As often was the case, they were trying to decide what to do with the day.

"We can't go to the beach because of the sharks," Sally said as she listed the various possibilities. "We can't go to the lighthouse because we burned that down. We can't go to the reservoir because we burned that as well. And we can't go to the Haunted Cave because it's haunted." She paused. "Maybe we should try to contact Ekwee12 and go for another ride on a flying saucer."

Watch shook his head. "We forgot to get a communication device from him. We have no way to contact him."

"But he promised to call us someday," Adam said.

"Yes," Sally replied. "But he's an alien. They have a different perspective on time. Someday might be ten thousand years from now for him."

"I thought you didn't like Ekwee12," Cindy said to Sally. "You kept calling him Fat Head."

"I called him that because he had a fat head," Sally said. "That does not mean I disliked him. I call you plenty of names and I still like you." Sally added, "Most of the time."

Cindy was not impressed. "I am *so* relieved."

"What if we didn't do anything special today?" Adam suggested. "What if we just hung out and relaxed? We could play checkers or chess or something."

Sally stared at him as if he had lost his mind. "Are you all right, Adam?"

"I'm fine," he said. "Just because I want to have a relaxing day doesn't mean there's anything wrong with me."

"But this is Spooksville," Sally said. "We don't relax here. That's the best way to get yourself killed. You always have to be on your guard."

"I don't see how playing chess could be dangerous," Adam said. "Even in Spooksville."

"Ha," Sally said, turning to Watch. "Tell him what happened to Sandy Stone."

Watch frowned. "We're not sure if the game did it to her."

"Of course we are," Sally said. "She was playing on the witch's chess board when it happened."

"What happened to her?" Cindy asked.

Sally shrugged. "She turned to stone. What would you expect with a name like Sandy Stone?"

"Is that true?" Adam asked Watch.

Watch appeared uncertain. "Well, we did find a stone

statue of Sandy not far from the witch's castle. And the statue was sitting in front of a mysterious-looking chess-board."

"I don't understand," Cindy said.

"Chess was Sandy's favorite game," Sally explained. "She was a master at it. She could beat anyone in town. The trouble was, she boasted about the fact, and apparently Ms. Witch Ann Templeton heard about it and didn't like it. The witch plays chess herself, and sent out a challenge to Sandy, which Sandy accepted." Sally paused and shook her head. "And that was the last any of us saw her alive."

"Are you saying the witch turned her to stone because Sandy lost to her?" Adam asked.

"It may have been because Sandy beat the witch," Sally said. "The witch is a well-known sore loser."

"Is the stone statue still there?" Cindy asked.

"No," Watch said. "It was made of soft stone, like compressed sand. The first good storm and it was gone. Down the gutter."

Cindy glanced at Adam. "Do you believe this?" she asked.

Adam shrugged. "Ms. Ann Templeton never seemed that bad to me."

Sally snorted. "Just because she's pretty and smiled

at you, Adam, you're willing to forgive years of murder and genocide."

"What does genocide mean?" Adam asked Watch.

"Unpleasant behavior toward many people," Watch explained.

"I can't believe she'd murder anyone," Adam said.

Sally threw back her head and laughed. "You're too much! What about those friendly troll bodyguards of hers we met in her cellar? Have you forgotten how they tried to spear us for dinner? Do you think they were just playing? Do you think she didn't approve of their hunting habits?"

"But it was Ann Templeton who gave Bum and me clues about how to find you guys while you were trapped in the Haunted Cave," Watch said.

"Yeah," Adam said. "She also gave Watch the magic words that helped us rescue the Hyeet from the cave. How do you explain that?"

Sally replied with exaggerated patience. "She told Watch how to get into the cave because she figured there was no way he'd get out. She probably told him the magic word because she was hoping we'd all get trapped in another dimension."

"But when the Cold People attacked," Adam said, "she was one of the few people who really tried to fight them off."

"She was trying to save her own skin," Sally said. "Nothing else."

"For once I have to agree with Sally," Cindy said reluctantly. "I saw those trolls she keeps in her basement. She must be an evil witch to have such monsters in her castle."

"Not necessarily," Adam said. "She might just feel sorry for them. I imagine trolls have trouble finding places to live."

Sally stared at him. "I can't believe you just said that. Her castle may be many things, but it is not a home for homeless trolls."

"I've never actually seen her hurt anyone with my own eyes," Watch said.

"Yeah, but you're half blind," Sally said. "You've never actually seen the sun come up."

"I can see the sun," Watch said quietly, perhaps hurt by the remark. "I can see the moon, too, as long as I have my glasses on."

"A lot of these stories about people dying and disappearing," Adam said, "might have nothing to do with her. They might be caused by natural creatures, like aliens and ghosts and things."

"But if she isn't evil," Cindy said to Adam, "why is everyone so afraid of her?"

Adam shrugged. "People believe all kinds of nasty rumors." He added, "You know, she invited me to her castle once."

"But even you weren't dumb enough to accept her invitation," Sally said. "Which just proves my point. Deep inside you know she'd just as soon eat your heart out as smile at you."

"That's not true," Adam said. "The only reason I haven't visited her at her castle is because I've been too busy since I moved here."

"You're not busy today," Sally mocked.

"I wouldn't mind visiting her at her castle," Watch said softly, almost to himself. "I've heard she has the power to heal. I've always wondered if she could do anything about my eyes."

To everyone's surprise, Sally reached over and squeezed Watch's hand. "Your eyes are fine the way they are," she said. "You don't need to be healed by that witch. I shouldn't have said what I did about your vision. I'm sorry, Watch."

Cindy glanced at Adam. "I can't believe Sally just apologized," she said.

"I've seen her do it once before," Adam said.

Sally spoke seriously to all of them. "No one's going to the castle. There are alligators and crocodiles in her moat that would eat you alive before you could even get inside. Believe me, the place is a death trap."

"But there's a drawbridge," Watch said. "If she wants us to enter, she'll let it down."

Adam studied Watch. "You really do want to go, don't you? Do your eyes bother you that much?"

Watch looked away, out the window of the ice-cream parlor. "Well, you know, I don't like to complain."

"Complain," Adam said. "You're with friends. How are your eyes?"

"I don't know," Watch said. Briefly he removed his glasses and cleaned them on his shirt. When he put them back on, he squinted in the distance. "I think they're getting worse."

Cindy was concerned. "Can't you get stronger glasses?"

Watch spoke reluctantly. Clearly the subject embarrassed him. "The doctors say no. You see, it's not just a focusing problem. Everything seems to be getting dimmer, like it's always evening."

"How is it at nighttime?" Adam asked.

"I can't really see then at all," Watch said. "Not anymore. I just bump into things."

Sally was worried. "You never told us."

Watch shook his head. "There's nothing you guys can do."

"But you should have told Ekwee12," Cindy said. "Remember the way he fixed my ankle with his healing machine?"

"They weren't as bad then," Watch said. "And I didn't want to bother him."

"Watch," Adam said, frustrated. "He's our friend. He would have been happy to help you."

Watch lowered his head. "Well, he's gone now. And we don't know when he'll be coming back."

"But maybe Ann Templeton can help you," Adam said. "I think it's worth the risk to ask her. Why don't we do that now?"

"Do what?" Cindy asked.

"Go to the castle," Adam said simply.

Sally and Cindy looked at each other. "The boys have lost their minds," Sally said.

"They're looking for help in all the wrong places," Cindy agreed.

"You two don't have to come," Adam said. "If you're scared."

"I'm not scared," Sally said. "I am just a reasonable thinking human being. Calling on evil witches—even in the middle of the day—is just plain stupid. She won't heal Watch's eyes. More likely, she'll carve them out with one of her long red nails and have them in her evening soup."

"She wouldn't have such a terrible reputation if she hadn't done something bad," Cindy agreed.

"I trust my own instincts," Adam said. "I think she's a good witch. What do you say, Watch?"

Watch nodded enthusiastically. "I want to visit her. I think she'll welcome us, especially since she's already invited you."

"This is going to be a long day," Sally said darkly.

Looking for another great book?
Find it in the middle.

in
the
middle
BOOKS

Fun, fantastic books for kids
in the in-beTWEEN age.

IntheMiddleBooks.com